MISSING
PRESUMED
MISSING

Paul Harris

Matador
Unit E2 Airfield Business Park,
Harrison Road, Market Harborough,
Leicestershire. LE16 7UL
Tel: 0116 2792299
Email: books@troubador.co.uk
Web: www.troubador.co.uk/matador
Twitter: @matadorbooks

ISBN 978 1803132 075

British Library Cataloguing in Publication Data.
A catalogue record for this book is available from the British Library.

Printed and bound in Great Britain by 4edge Limited
Typeset in 12pt Minion Pro by Troubador Publishing Ltd, Leicester, UK

Matador is an imprint of Troubador Publishing Ltd

For my wife Robyn and daughter Laura x

To Judith Paskin, whose support and encouragement
was invaluable

PROLOGUE

Robert glances at the clock on his bedside cabinet.
He ponders whether he should go to school today. It's Tuesday and so no history.

He slowly rolls out of bed, stopping in front of the mirror.

Smoothing his slick hair behind his ears, Robert tilts his head slightly. He poses for a few seconds, moving his face closer to the mirror.

He runs a finger over his protruding nose.

Slowly, he lumbers away from his reflection.

He tugs his shirt down into his trousers and fastens the buttons. He smooths down a hint of a crease in the white fabric.

He gazes at the sea of orange-shirt pictures sprinkled across his bedroom wall, above his bed. They are all famous Dutch footballers. His dad lives in

Holland and he'd spent a holiday there last year with him.

Robert trundles down the stairs and into the hallway. He seizes his school shoes, scrutinises them and decides they need a touch of polish.

He ambles through the lounge and glances at his mum, who is sitting on the settee, still in her pyjamas. She's reading a magazine, a cup of coffee in her hand.

He grabs the last carton of milk from the fridge.

'I'll be out when you get back from school,' she calls out to him. 'Make yourself beans on toast or something.'

Robert stops pouring his milk and looks puzzled. 'Where are you going?'

'Oh, just out to see a friend. They live a good way away, so I'll be late back,' she replies.

He walks back through to the lounge and sits down, carefully balancing his full bowl of cereal on his knees.

Picking up his school history book from a side table, he opens the book and starts to read.

That's the signal for Mungo to meander towards Robert, her tail wagging. She brushes up against his legs as he swallows a mouthful of cereal.

'Go away! You've had your breakfast!' Robert says, pushing the dog away.

'No, she hasn't,' says his mum, her gaze still fixed on her magazine.

'She gets her hairs all over my books,' Robert protests.

'Oh, don't be so precious!' she sneers. 'Anyway, you should put them away safely. It's not her fault.'

Robert sighs. 'We're down to the last carton of milk, by the way.'

'Can you pick some up on your way home? Won't take you long,' she says, slowly turning the page.

'But I go through the woods, nowhere near the shop!'

'You might as well live in those woods. Trees, more trees, and guess what, more trees!' his mum says sarcastically. 'You can call in the shop later when you take Mungo for a walk.'

Robert shakes his head. 'I was going to play football with a mate later.'

'Well, you can miss it for once, can't you?' She pulls a face. 'The dog will need a walk!'

'Can't you do it?' Robert asks.

She slams the magazine down on the floor. 'No, I can't!' she shouts. 'You're fifteen! Not too old to do as you're told!'

Robert reluctantly offers a few cornflakes to Mungo before disappearing into the kitchen to drop his bowl into the sink. He'll wash it later.

He grabs his orange scarf off the back of the door and wraps it twice around his neck.

Picking up his books, he moves into the hallway, before picking up his coat.

He slams the door behind him and strides away from the house, turning left at the end of the drive.

He'll go through the woods on his way to school.

Leaden clouds scud across the sky above him. He bundles the books underneath his coat; it looks like rain.

The early-morning mist hasn't lifted; it hangs heavy around the woods. He treads carefully along a track that leads into the woods. He doesn't want to muddy his shoes.

He moves swiftly over to where he'd begun to make a shelter a couple of nights before. There are a couple of old blankets he'd brought from home to make a den.

He feels a sense of peace here in the woods. He might stay out here a bit later tonight if it keeps dry. No point in rushing home.

He takes out a small penknife from the inside pocket of his jacket. Peeling away the bark of a younger tree, he gathers the strips of wood, hiding them under a carpet of leaves. They'd be useful for making a small fire to keep him warm, if it got cold later.

The wind feels like it's getting stronger as it whistles through the trees. The autumn chill seeps into his bones as Robert swings his scarf tightly around his neck. The dampness is slowly evaporating in the early-morning sunshine, but the ground is hard.

The leaves are crisp, and crunch beneath his feet as he walks.

Stillness descends upon the woods; the only sound he can hear is birdsong.

Suddenly he lurches backwards as the scarf snags on a prickly bush.

He briefly examines his scarf, noting a small thread has come loose. He tucks the scarf snugly inside his coat.

Winding his way past several small shrubs and bushes, he suddenly stops in his tracks. A low murmuring echoes around him. It's coming from the ground!

The earth vibrates. The trees shake fervently, swaying from side to side. Robert turns his head, unsure what's happening.

He'll be late if he doesn't hurry.

As he looks ahead for the familiar path to the edge of the woods, he thinks he can see a pair of eyes behind a mass of bracken and undergrowth.

Probably someone walking their dog, he reckons. It's difficult to see properly in the half-light.

He creeps forward slowly, trying to get a better view of what's behind the bracken. He halts, his gaze fixed on the eyes, which haven't moved.

As he gets nearer, a bright, shimmering archway appears, lighting up the surrounding trees, turning them into a magical cavern.

He waits. Peering through tangled foliage, Robert blinks hard, squinting to make sure he isn't imagining the golden light.

He feels a strange magnetic pull towards the eyes.

He glances round, noticing the small bushes are quivering. Rustling leaves rub against each other, as if they are shaking.

He can hear a rumble. Like a drum. He looks down at the earth. It's pulsating, as though it's alive!

Robert fixes his gaze straight ahead, walking through clumps of mud. He steers a path towards the eyes.

Mungo would not get her walk that day.

ONE

Knock at the bedroom door.

Five o'clock.

I can hear the repetitive chirp from the bird clock in the kitchen.

'I'm not hungry, Mum.'

'It's your favourite, fish fingers and chips.' Her voice goes up an octave.

Five o'clock is a sacred time in our house. You could set Big Ben by Mum's punctuality.

'Come on, you don't want your dinner to go cold. I want to hear all about your day.'

'It's not my favourite,' I shout, sighing deeply, before pulling myself up from the bed.

I wait at the foot of the stairs and take a deep breath. At least the song thrush has stopped.

The fish fingers and chips are assembled on one of

her posh dinner plates. Mum sits in her chair, patiently waiting.

Mum's chair.

There's no label to say it's *her* chair, but she always makes a point of sitting in that seat. She says she can get out easier to answer the door or phone, if she sits there.

I plop down on one of the chairs, around the shiny oval table, which is so bright I can see the outline of my face in it.

She's got her favourite local radio station on.

'There you go. I expect you've been waiting for that.' She grins like a Cheshire cat, which I try to ignore.

'Anyway, you always say you like it, and you never leave anything on your plate.' She tilts her head to one side and looks at me expectantly.

'Not my favourite,' I quietly insist.

I lower my head and concentrate on the food. The polished surface of the table smells of disinfectant.

She tries to listen, I know. But she only listens to the things she *wants* to listen to. And we never really sit down and talk. Not about the important stuff.

'Well, what is?' she says, jerking her head back before disappearing into the next room to adjust the thermostat.

'What?'

'Your favourite?'

I shrug my shoulders and can't be bothered to think of anything else. But it's definitely not fish fingers and chips.

'It's getting colder now the clocks have gone back. You're not cold in your room, are you, Michael?' she says, before sitting down at the table again.

'No.'

'You don't want to catch a cold, especially after you've just started at a new school.'

'I'm fine.'

The kitchen blinds are closed, and the lounge curtains are partly drawn to screen out the fading sun.

It stops people who walk by peering through the window; they should mind their own business.

'Suppose it's to be expected, this time of year. Most of the leaves have already fallen off next door's trees.' She angles her head downwards towards my plate, encouraging me to eat.

I can feel her eyes boring down on me as I squirt sauce generously around the edge of the plate.

'I don't think that much sauce is good for you, Michael.'

I shovel in the food as quickly as I can and only have a couple of fish fingers left when suddenly Mum says enthusiastically, 'So, what happened today at school? Did you sit with anyone nice for lunch?'

The question seems to creep up undetected and assaults me, despite her efforts to make it sound as though this wasn't something she'd been planning to ask the whole day.

I always sit on my own at lunchtime. Once, I tried

going over to sit with Jamie Jones, but he just swivelled round and sat with his back towards me.

I didn't bother again after that.

'I don't really like those muesli bars, especially those almond ones you put in my lunch box,' I suddenly say.

'Oh, I thought you liked them. I thought they were one of your favourites.'

I'm pleased we're off the subject of school, but feel bad when I see the puzzled expression on her face.

'I've gone off them,' I explain.

'Well, you never said anything,' she says, dabbing her mouth with the serviette.

'I prefer the orange ones.'

'So did you eat it, or did you give it to someone else at lunchtime?'

I put my knife and fork down and stare at my last fish finger, hoping that it will jump into my mouth and save me from having to think about the lunch hour.

'I brought it back,' I say, rummaging around in a trouser pocket, before plonking it on the table.

'Oh, you could've given it to one of your friends.' She smiles. 'They might have liked it.'

I can see the gleam of hope in her bright blue eyes as she mentions the word friends. Perhaps she thinks you can just buy a friend in the supermarket, like you do fish fingers.

'I had my lunch later, and everyone had left by the time I got to the canteen.'

Now this wasn't strictly true, as there were a few older children around by the time I arrived, but most of them had left to have their lunch on the fields because it was such a warm day.

'Oh, why was that then?'

'Most of my year has eaten by one o'clock,' I say, picking my knife and fork up again.

'No, I mean, why were you so late for lunch?'

'Mr Logie stopped me to talk about local history.'

'But it made you late for lunch. Didn't he realise that?' Her voice starts to climb two octaves.

'He should know a growing twelve-year-old needs their meals on time. What's wrong with him?'

I like Mr Logie. He reminds me of a bald eagle on account of his beaky nose; though to be fair, he has thick black hair, which he combs back. More importantly, he's the sort of teacher who makes lessons fun. He joked once about the Battle of Hastings actually taking place at Battle, but said the Battle of Battle sounded confusing, which made us all laugh.

I don't even mind the mini-test he does at the end of each lesson. He is undoubtedly my favourite teacher.

Glancing up, I see Mum tossing the merits of education versus food around her mind. The last fish finger joins its friends.

'You dad will be home soon. Do you want to do anything tonight?'

I know what she's getting at. She wants us to play 'Kerplunk' or 'Operation' and sit around the table in the lounge, drinking hot chocolate and eating. Like normal families. Like when I was eight.

'I'm okay, Mum. Just a bit tired, that's all.'

'Perhaps a game of chess? Your father wants a rematch.' Her eyes nearly pop out of their sockets.

I begin slowly to inch out of the chair, giving her the chance to say something like, *Michael, you can't stay in your room all evening.*

I like my room. It's cosy and warm, and I can listen to my music and know I won't be disturbed.

'Don't you want a pudding? I could do a treacle sponge. It won't take long.'

'Not that hungry, thanks.'

'Perhaps later?' She nods enthusiastically.

'Maybe,' I say, smiling weakly, hoping we've finished.

Looking out of the door window, I spy a couple of children on their bikes doing wheelies. They zoom down the road before suddenly screeching to a halt, spinning round and standing their bikes up.

I've never had a bike.

I walk slowly up the stairs and close the door to my room. A little while later, I hear Dad's voice as he announces his arrival home from work.

'Oh, is that you? Dinner won't be long,' Mum shouts.

The volume on the radio has been turned up.

I press my ear to the door and can just about make out what's being said.

'So who's he been today – Jack Flash or Mole?'

'Mole,' she says.

'So he's not said much?'

'Hardly anything.'

'He needs his hair cut. Can you take him?'

'I suppose so.' She sounds irritated. 'You know how he hates going out to places where he might be seen,' she says.

'It's not normal. He's been at Longfields eight weeks now, and he hasn't made a single friend, talked about school, or anything.' Dad sounds weary.

'He did say he'd had a chat with Mr Logie, the history teacher, just now.'

'Oh, what about?' The despairing tone of Dad's voice leaves me in no doubt that he's not too impressed.

'Something about the local area. At least it's a start,' Mum says.

I can tell she's trying her best to convince Dad it's a step in the right direction.

'Mole, that's me!' A picture of a slithery, missile-shaped furry animal burrowing beneath the ground enters my mind.

Perhaps I'll be Jack Flash tomorrow.

TWO

'C'mon, Michael, it's half-past seven. You'll be late for school.' Mum's voice drifts up the stairs.

I feel drained. I didn't sleep well again.

Yes, it's half-past seven, but no, I won't be late for school. Five minutes is all it takes to throw on yesterday's blue shirt and a pair of black trousers that hang over the chair.

Five minutes.

I pause in front of the rectangular mirror, set in the oak wardrobe, staring at the unsmiling face that glowers back.

I wonder if Jack Flash has permanently disappeared.

My face is too long and my chin too pointy. The top of my head is even worse, with its clump of dark, tangled hair, like a haystack, crowning my pale skin.

The rest of me is a work in progress. I hope. My body

seems to just hang there, propping up my growing head and trying to hang on to the dangly legs, which seem to flop about like Bambi on ice.

Trying to straighten or make my hair sit flat is impossible; the hairbrush hovers above the black mop, as a token weapon.

It does need cutting.

I grab a pen off my desk and strike another day off the wall calendar. It's only two more weeks till an inset day. When I can just stay in and not bother with anything, or anyone.

I'm never late for school anyway.

I know Mum would be mortally wounded if I racked up an absent mark against the name of Michael Dobson.

I bet she had days off school.

I cringe when I think back to my first week, and her offer to walk me to school on my first day.

As I near the bottom of the stairs, I see the shoes neatly stacked in the shoe rack. Mum cleans all of them every night, before we go to bed.

There are two piles of magazines and old newspapers on the coffee table in the middle of the lounge. One stack has football magazines for Dad. I think he hopes I'll read them, but I don't like football. I'm sure he's disappointed.

Family photographs adorn the mantelpiece and windowsill. Mum cleans them every day.

I don't like having my photo taken.

Looking at them, I can still feel Mum's gentle nudge in my back, forcing me to smile.

Mum doesn't work. She'd like to work from home, rather than work in an office. She can drive, but I've never seen her drive our car. She doesn't like public transport. Seriously limits her options.

So now she stays at home. Cleaning, and making notes.

'Eat your muesli and I'll get you some juice,' Mum says.

'Can we have cornflakes?'

'Muesli is better for you, Michael. It's got more in it.' She's gone to the kitchen cupboard and returns with the packet.

'I prefer cornflakes.'

She scans the list of ingredients and starts to read it out. 'Oats and hazelnuts...' She turns the box round on the table, so I see it.

Then she's gone off again to get the orange juice.

'Anyway, we haven't got time to argue. Otherwise, you'll be late for school. You don't want to be marked absent, do you? What lessons have you got today?' She returns with a glass of orange juice.

'Double English in the morning, and history in the afternoon,' I say.

'Oh, I expect you'll be doing one of the classics this year, like *Great Expectations*. We did that in Year Seven, when I was at school. We even saw the film in class.'

'Mr Logie has organised a league table in history, and you get to pick a team,' I say, wiping the dregs of juice from my mouth.

Mum suddenly stops in her tracks. 'What's the point of that? I thought it was a history lesson,' she says.

'It is. We have a test at the end of each lesson and, depending on your result, you go up or down the league table. Get it?'

'I'm not sure about that,' she says, and a frown clouds her face. 'I'll make a note for parents' evening.'

Not looking forward to that.

She begins to fill my lunch box with the sandwiches she prepared the previous evening.

'I don't want an almond bar, remember,' I shout through to the kitchen.

She's busy writing a note about Mr Logie's lessons and carries on scribbling, even when I appear at the kitchen door.

Mum makes notes about everything. It's intensely irritating. She sits there, her pen poised, as she thinks about what to put in the note. I watch her, pen raised to her lips, as she stares into space, waiting for some kind of inspiration before scribbling something down. You can almost see the wires connecting as she struggles to find the exact words.

I turn and am making my way to the hallway, when she rushes up behind me to give me my shoes.

'I've given them a good polish. Try and keep them clean. Oh, by the way, shall I make an appointment for you to have your hair cut later today, Michael? It won't take long.'

Not a good idea. She knows how I hate getting my hair cut. I have to move like lightning, to get in the car, then get out and run across the street to the hairdresser's. There are people out there, people who've never seen me, and I don't like them watching me and making things up about me. At least they know me in the hairdresser's, and I can get my clump cut quickly. I just don't feel right.

Mole doesn't feel safe.

'Couldn't they come to us, you know, like a mobile hairdresser?' I suggest.

'It won't take longer than half an hour. You'll be in and out before you know it.'

'Make it later after school, about five-ish,' I say, grabbing my blazer from the cloakroom.

'What about your tea?'

'We could have tea afterwards,' I say, shoving the lunch box into the bag and slinging the bag over my shoulder.

'But tea is always at five. We could get your hair cut before that.'

I glance at the clock above the fridge. 'I'll be late. I don't want to be late. Bye,' I say, kissing her on the cheek. She grabs my shoulders to hug me.

She releases me quickly, before picking up a pen and making a note about getting my hair cut later today.

'Oh, by the way, Uncle Steven is coming on Tuesday,' Mum says.

Mum's older brother.

'Is he, great!' I smile. Uncle Steven is the best. 'How is he?' half turning towards her.

'Oh, much the same,' Mum says indifferently.

'You never know, he might walk again one day if they get his legs better,' I suggest.

'No, the doctors said it's permanent.' Mum's voice has an air of resignation. 'He hasn't been too good lately.' A tinge of sadness fills her voice.

Mum's probably right. Uncle Steven will never walk again.

'Oh, and close the gate, will you, Michael. Other people's sweet papers and rubbish always lands in our garden.'

I am halfway up the littered garden, and out of the gate, as Mum finishes her sentence.

The two hundred-yard walk to school has started.

I can be at school or home within five minutes. I think that was one of the things that decided it for Mum and Dad when we moved here, just before the summer. Longfields had a good reputation, and was five minutes away from the house.

Mum's actually been to school once already this term. She was called in when Miss Pearson reported me to the school nurse, because she thought there was something wrong with me.

Miss Pearson had asked us to get into groups for drama. I couldn't move or speak. I get hot and sweaty at just the idea of being in a group. I couldn't say a word, just couldn't. So she sent me to the nurse, who rang Mum.

I hate drama.

Good job it's only once a fortnight.

Up ahead, I see the pavement is relatively clear, apart from Sue Nicholls and Abi Linton, who are walking arm in arm, like they don't have a care in the world.

They move from one side of the pavement to the other; it looks like they're doing synchronised pavement dancing. Right foot over left and then the other way; then they have a fit of giggles as they collide and nearly fall over.

I keep my head down, distracting myself by trying to avoid the cracks in the paving stones. I try and steer clear of the tufts of grass springing up between the cracks.

Not many people about. They've probably gone to work; most people use their cars. The man who lives two doors down from me walks past me with his dog. He smiles, so I just smile back.

Anyway, five minutes is all it takes.

Those girls are getting closer now; they've slowed to a crawl, and they're now looking at one another's nails.

I could speed up, do a slick manoeuvre, and pass them on the outside.

They've stopped and formed a huddle, blocking the whole pavement. There are fences on one side and a grassed area on the other.

Now!

I feel a surge of adrenalin and skilfully shoot past

them, accelerating in a near-perfect move, before steering back onto the pavement.

I turn into the road that leads to Longfields and keep to the side, as bikes suddenly whizz by.

I can relax more now we're in the school grounds.

The steps and entrance to the doors are ahead. I can see Jonty Johnson and his cronies gathered together, at the foot of the steps. They're laughing and throwing their arms around. Jonty has one of his mates in a headlock. I wince as he tightens his grip on his victim by exaggerating a turn of his muscular arm.

Jonty swivels the boy in the headlock round, till he's facing me. He grins at me and his large stained molars are bared.

'All right, Dobbin, what's stable life like then, eh?' he bellows, forcing me to offer a weak smile in his direction.

I watch as his mates all laugh like a pack of hyenas. I quicken my step, hoping to put distance between us.

Most of my form is already here, and Mr Jones is sitting at his desk, playing with his moustache, engrossed in the book he's reading.

Registration.

Melanie Smithson sits next to me. She smiles as I sit down. I politely nod to her, before taking a pen out of my bag.

'Have you looked at the prose yet?' she asks.

'No! I didn't think it was due till Thursday!' I exclaim, and suddenly my heart's thumping, and beads of sweat race to the surface of my skin.

'Is it *today*?'

Melanie Smithson has this annoying habit of not answering you when you ask her something. Like now.

She can see the panic rising in me, and it seems to be an eternity before she answers.

'No, just asking, that's all,' she says, and turns to start a conversation with Ben Gillet. He lives near Melanie Smithson. They knew each other before Longfields.

As I silently curse her, I turn to see who's coming through the door, and Jonty breezes in, and pushes his fist against my cheek.

'Well, stable boy?'

'Fine,' I answer. Not sure if this is what he wants to hear.

Jonty leans over me, his back to Mr Jones. He pushes his fist against the side of my mouth, and I feel my mouth dribbling.

I reach for a handkerchief, but Jonty snatches it from me. He prises my mouth open and stuffs it in. I start to cough uncontrollably, and hope Mr Jones isn't watching. It'll only make things worse.

No one's watching.

Jonty claps both hands against my cheeks. I'm gasping for breath and try to pull the wet handkerchief out.

He pinches my cheek with his thumb and forefinger, making a whirring noise, like he's drilling into my gums.

He straightens up and lightly slaps my face with the back of his hand as he moves away.

'See you at break time, Dobbin.'

My heart sinks, and I feel sick.

I freeze, unable to do anything, unaware of anything else going on around me.

I just wait for the moment to wash over me.

Mole will stay in the library and keep his head down.

It'll be all right.

THREE

A short cut.

I've been this way a few times.

There's still light; it won't get dark for a few hours.

Most of my class live on the other side of school, so they don't come this way.

There's no sign of Jonty. I can relax. I'll probably be home the same time as usual.

Some of the trees have lost their leaves. They stand there naked, shivering. Mum says I feel the cold, but I'm wearing a thick coat, so no problem.

The path is wet from the afternoon's rain. It's muddy in places. I step away from the clumps of mud so as not to get my shoes dirty. Mum wouldn't be happy.

The crunching of twigs beneath my feet is the only sound in the woods as I follow the path that leads to my house.

I swerve to avoid brushing against some bushes. The air feels damp. The light is beginning to fail.

Need to quicken my step.

The wind suddenly picks up and nearly blows me off my feet. It's getting colder and I pull my jacket tighter.

It's round to the right, and then more or less straight ahead.

Only, the path looks slightly different than usual… it must be the gathering gloom. The colours around me seem to change – orange and brown – and a golden arc of bright light bends to touch the forest floor.

A sudden gust of wind springs up and catches the trees. Their branches stoop down, waving me forward.

The trees are bending in different directions, as though they're suddenly awake.

The rustling of the leaves causes me to panic slightly. It's like they're chattering.

I spot a clearing slightly to the left.

This will take me to the grassy bank next to the road, near the house.

At first, the path goes in a straight line and everything's fine. Looking up ahead, I can see some big trees, but there are big gaps between them. That's where I need to go.

I screw my eyes tighter to make sure I keep to the track. The light's beginning to fade.

I check my watch. I need to get a move on. Pulling my phone out of my pocket, I'm relieved to see no missed calls or messages.

What's wrong with the stupid path? How can I be lost? I've done this route a dozen times before. I'm tempted to go back. I will have to run to make up time.

I start to jog. But every direction seems to bring me back to the same point. I'm going round in a circle!

The swaying trees move rhythmically from side to side. It's like a frenzied dance. I stop and watch.

I'm going to be late home if I don't hurry! The last of the daylight has almost disappeared. Perhaps I should turn back and take the normal way home from school.

A squirrel darts across my path. I suddenly pull up and catch my breath.

But slightly beyond, hovering above an unwieldy mass of undergrowth, is a soft, shimmery silvery light. It lights up the darkness.

I rub my eyes to make sure the fading sun is not playing tricks. I've seen paintings where colours merge and make everything look unreal. Like an illusion.

We're too far from the road. It can't be the light from the lamp posts.

It may be a torch or some shiny object.

The ground pulsates with invisible energy. I can hear a throbbing noise coming from under my feet! But it's no ordinary sound.

There's a shape shrouded in the undergrowth, but I can't make it out. Only the light is visible. It's so bright.

It's someone local, I hope. They'll know the way out. I hope they're friendly. I'm only asking for directions.

I'm starting to feel hungry now. Mum will be starting tea.

This should only take a minute.

The branches wave and flap about, willing me to go on.

I keep my gaze on the light as it filters through the trees. It's getting brighter, more like a glare.

There's an open space around two large beech trees. They stand tall and strong, like columns, their trailing branches forming an archway. The light shines through like an illuminated entrance to a grotto.

I feel the brush of a few shaking leaves against my legs. They make a gentle whirring sound. I look underneath the bushes and the ground vibrates. The energy beneath my feet intensifies.

The whole area is jumping around, lifting my feet. I feel like I'm in a fast-flowing river, being carried along – I'm heading towards the archway… and I can't stop myself.

My nose is twitchy. The air smells musty, like the mothballs you find among unworn clothes in an old person's wardrobe.

Peering through the glistening foliage, I grasp an outline through the dense undergrowth.

The figure isn't moving. The dazzling light seems to emanate from their eyes.

The eyes lock on me.

The area is literally flooded with light. I hold a hand above my eyes to combat the glare.

I slowly approach the figure, when all of a sudden I feel a firm hand grasp my arm.

'Aargh, get off!' I shout, tugging at the arm. But the hand has a firm grip.

I twist, thrusting my arm forward. The hand grips my arm tighter.

'Let go!' I scream.

I shake my arm up and down frantically.

I see someone moving about ahead. They might be able to help me.

There's a huge lump in my throat. I can't get any words out. Please help me!

I feel hot, and my body has gone limp. The hand gripping my arm is much stronger. I can't get away.

With a final heave, I lurch towards the eyes and light. It's my only chance.

'Got you, Dobbin boy!' Jonty has his chubby arm wrapped round my neck.

'Told you I'd catch up with you, you squirt bag.'

I close my eyes, waiting for his fist to start pummelling my head.

I should have gone the normal way home.

Falling forward, we both fall through a gap in the undergrowth and onto a patch of dry grass. Jonty suddenly releases me. He thrusts my nose into the ground for good measure.

I keep perfectly still. I hope he's stopped giving me his undivided attention. For now.

Still, at least I can stretch out a bit, now that he's released me.

Slowly looking up, the first thing I feel is being really warm.

I spot Jonty's size nines a few feet away.

The trees look listless, branches hanging limply by the side of their trunks.

I quickly glance at Jonty. He seems to have forgotten about me for the present.

I'm shocked to see an old woman standing next to Jonty. She's dressed in a black cloak and leaning on a staff.

Her face is dried up, her skin shrivelled. There are lines across her forehead, and her cheeks are sunken. I wonder if she's homeless – maybe she lives in the woods.

Mum tells me not to speak to strangers.

I scrunch my eyes, as it's quite bright here; sunny even, which is a bit odd. It was nearly dark just a few minutes before.

The woman's gnarled hand rests on Jonty's shoulder. She pats him like you would a dog.

They're whispering. They seem an odd couple. Jonty towers over her like some giant and he's actually listening to her. She's unlike any old lady I've ever seen. She tilts her head to one side as she talks; it looks like she's trying to convince Jonty of something.

Her arched back slowly straightens, as though she's

heard some good news! She lifts her shoulders and holds her head high. She's almost level with Jonty's eyes now. Then I see her eyes. They gleam even in the brightness.

Was she the person walking in the woods?

I lay perfectly still, trying to work out what's just happened.

I daren't move, but I can hear other voices, some distance away.

My brain tries to make sense of it all. Jonty must have seen me and followed me into the woods. I need to get away from here. I need to get home.

The sun is shining, and there's not a cloud in the sky. It's like daytime. But it should be evening. I move my head slowly round and catch my breath.

Where am I?

The drooping branches of the trees spring to life once again, as if waking from their winter hibernation. They look stronger, more solid.

I catch the sound of laughter. The sweet smell of cut grass drifts through the air.

If I crouch low and stay quiet, I can find a way out of here. I've got to sneak past Jonty first, then run until I find the way out.

I slip away, crouching low, almost on all fours. That's how Mole would escape.

I retrace my steps, quietly slipping away. I can see the two big beech trees. They actually seem closer together from what I remember. They block my way. There's only a narrow gap to slide through.

I creep through the beech trees, darting away as fast as my legs will carry me.

Whoa! It's suddenly dark! The trees loom large, their branches draped over the path.

It's biting cold.

In the skyline, I can make out lights from a block of flats, near to where I live.

I look over my shoulder. Jonty isn't following me. I breathe a huge sigh of relief.

I snag my trousers on a thorny bush as I finally arrive on the grassy verge at the side of the road. A passing car honks at me, warning me to be careful before crossing the road.

I pause, looking back at the woods.

Strangely, Mr Logie's large beak fills my mind.

My head is fuzzy and I'm totally confused.

What just happened in there?

FOUR

The class is milling outside the history classroom as Mr Logie climbs the stairs that link the west wing of the school to the long corridor down below.

He's near the top of the stairs, and the rest of the class start to form a single file as he turns the corner.

I move away from the few steps that lead to the door as the class jostle for places. Harrison and Pierce squeeze and twist their fists into the backs of those in front of them. I'm glad I'm standing at the back.

Jonty Johnson isn't here yet.

We file into the classroom behind Mr Logie. A small group gathers around the big league table that's pinned on the wall next to the door. Fingers run up and down to find their team.

I know I'm in fourth place, so I don't need to check. That's going to change this week.

Melanie Smithson is already seated at her desk, her face composed and her head held high. She annoys me intensely. Everything about her is neat. She's always immaculately dressed; it's like she's got a maid to press and iron her school uniform every morning. Her nails are dead smooth, like a skating rink; her fingers are dainty and delicate.

She has trim, brown shoulder-length hair, and her skin looks as smooth as a baby's bottom. Or whatever. She seems oblivious to the cacophony of noise that swirls around the room, acting super cool, and in her own little world.

We wait for Mr Logie.

My feet are bobbing about underneath the desk, and my heels bounce up and down on the tiled floor.

We're getting the results of the mini-test we did last week. I fancy my chances, especially as I'd read all about the First World War the night before.

Mr Logie leans against his desk at the front and his razor-like eyes peer around the room. He wearing an orange scarf that's so long, it almost touches the floor.

He's holding a piece of paper and waiting for the hum of chatter to die down.

Suddenly the room becomes eerily quiet.

There's a space next to Harrison where Jonty usually sits.

Mr Logie nods his head to show he's ready.

I'm itching to know how I did in the test. You can hardly hear a pin drop as he clears his throat.

I feel my heart pumping, and wonder why there isn't a drum roll as the results will soon begin.

Jack Flash is cock-a-hoop and confident, standing tall, as I bounce up and down in my seat waiting for the result.

Mr Logie is ever so slightly dramatic for a history teacher; he pauses for what feels like an hour before he starts to announce names.

A sombre expression clouds his face as his booming voice begins the roll call.

'In twenty-sixth place…' He waits four seconds before he reads out 'Harrison's Heroes.' He looks in the direction of Jonty's friend Harrison, as if to say, *you can do better*.

'Jonty Giants are in twenty-fifth place,' he continues. A low murmur envelops the room.

But I can't contain myself, and whoop loudly at this news. I swerve to take cover behind several heads.

Mr Logie looks my way, but I duck my head.

Harrison eyes me.

Melanie Smithson raises her eyebrows, but I'm not bothered.

It won't be me for ages.

I'm confident Wizard's Troops will be in the top three. I'll be going up the league table this week.

And last week's test wasn't that difficult.

I'm tapping my fingers on the desk, as the waiting game is almost unbearable. Mr Logie reaches the top ten; my name hasn't been read yet.

Nor has Melanie Smithson's.

I glance across at her, but she doesn't seem to be excited, although you can never tell by looking at her.

I sway from side to side, trying to catch the eye of Mr Logie.

My bottom's beginning to lose contact with the seat as I squeeze my eyes shut, willing Mr Logie to skip the rest of the class and go straight to number one.

I open my eyes and glance sideways. Melanie Smithson pretends not to notice me rocking from side to side.

I've rehearsed my victory celebrations, and my heart must be literally pumping millions of pints of blood as third place is announced.

I allow a smile to settle on my lips, and I feel all eyes are now firmly fixed on me, even though they're not.

Jack Flash is coming to the party.

'In second place is Michael Dobson.'

Mr Logie smiles and nods approvingly at me, but somebody has just ripped my mask off, and I'm floating down to earth.

I clap for Melanie Smithson, along with the others, as she blushes slightly at the enthusiastic cheering, even from Harrison.

'Well done, you did really well,' she says, leaning across. I'm sure she means it.

'And you,' I reply, but my words are half-hearted, and I know I can't hide my disappointment.

Ben Gillet is holding his hands out as though he can't believe the result. 'Great Goliath' wasn't even in the top half of the class.

As everyone troops out of the classroom, I wait to see Mr Logie.

'Anything wrong, Michael?' he asks.

'Not really,' I mumble, moving closer to his desk.

'That was a good effort,' he says, and smiles. 'It won't be long before you're challenging for that top place.'

'Mmm,' I nod.

I could have done better in the test. Melanie Smithson must have got all the questions right.

Not sure how to start this.

'I'm glad you like history, Michael. That's great. It can help us look at things from the past and make sense of the present. It can also solve all sorts of mysteries.'

'What sort of mysteries, sir?' I begin tentatively.

'Oh, you know, things we can't explain. Things that defy logic,' he muses.

'Sir, do you know anything about the history of Spinney Wood?' I ask.

He stoops and moves his head closer; his pointed nose almost reaches my face. I steel myself to not lean away from him.

'Spinney Wood, eh? The local history archives say it used to be a burial site in the Neolithic period,' he says.

'Burial site?' I say guardedly.

Mr Logie has got quite a big head, and I flinch slightly as I picture a sharp beak clawing at my skin.

'Only, we live close by,' I add.

He narrows his eyes slightly. 'What about Spinney Wood?' he asks.

'Did you find anything else out, sir?'

He quickly gathers his books and papers and glances at the big clock on the wall.

'The whole area used to be part of a forest where the ancient tribe of Laco once lived,' he says, his tone clipped.

His beady eyes look straight at me.

He glances over my head towards the door. We're alone.

'The tribe was wiped out. That's about as much as I know,' he finishes.

I swallow hard and take a deep breath.

'So, like in a battle?'

Mr Logie looks away to collect his thoughts. A forlorn look suddenly clouds his face.

'Best to stay away from Spinney Wood,' he says.

He looks troubled. I may have upset him.

I need to leave, as it's the end of the day, and I know Mum will be anxious if I'm late. She'll be texting me to ask if something has happened, and if I'm all right.

I think I've heard enough. I wriggle away slowly.

'Well done again, Michael, in the test,' he says suddenly.

I notice his hands are gripping his papers mid-air, his knuckles white.

I glance out of the window. Kids are on their way home. I've never been this late before.

I turn back to Mr Logie, who looks really upset. His eyes have glazed over, like he's going to cry. What's he getting so emotional about? I'm starting to feel very uncomfortable.

Glad I'm leaving.

'Er, I really have to go now, Mr Logie. Thanks.'

I turn quickly and move away.

'Keep up the good work,' he says.

I slip out of the classroom and into the hallway, where Harrison is waiting.

I stop in my tracks and take a big gulp as he rushes at me, pushing me against one of the lockers.

'What was that stupid noise when my mate's name was read out, horsey boy?'

'I got carried away, sorry,' I start, hoping I can arouse some sympathy. As if.

Harrison is big and the corridor is almost empty. He towers over me, hiding me from any onlookers.

I feel panicky and my mouth is getting dry. My feet are leaden, and my eyes are jumping from side to side, searching for help.

'You seen Jonty?' he asks, grabbing my collar. He cups my chin tightly in his outstretched hand.

'Yesterday,' I say.

'Only, he said he was going to follow you home,' says Harrison with one of his evil grins.

I try to straighten my back, as it's pinned against the locker, but it's too much effort. I feel trapped.

As Harrison glances up the corridor, a shrill voice pipes up on the other side.

'Mr Logie would give you detention if he knew what you were doing.' Melanie Smithson stands as near to Harrison's toes as she can get.

Harrison's smile suddenly disappears.

Melanie Smithson puts her hands on her hips. 'I'm not waiting here forever. I've got a home to go to even if you haven't.'

Harrison shakes my chin from side to side in a violent wave.

Finally letting go, he shoves his face within a whisker of mine. 'We haven't finished with you, Dobbin. See you around.' He flicks his hand across my cheek.

As he turns and walks down the corridor, I straighten my collar, while clearing my throat and pulling my jumper down.

'Thanks.' The word slowly drips out of my mouth.

Melanie Smithson just stands there with a big smile on her face.

'Harrison and Johnson are always throwing their weight around. Good job I saw you were still with Mr Logie. I knew you were upset. You shouldn't be; you did your best.'

I feel as though she's twisting the knife in deeper and deeper, waiting to pick up my entrails as they spill out on the ground.

'I did okay. I didn't have much time last week to revise, so it's no big deal,' I counter.

'Wizard's Troops!' she says with an incredulous look. 'What sort of name is that anyway?'

'Better than Melony Magic,' I joke, pleased we've got the conversation back to name-calling.

I wait, wishing she would just disappear, so I can get off home. I don't want to be seen with a girl after school, but she just stands there, arms still folded.

Harrison appears to be long gone, though I still have the walk home to negotiate. He might still be hovering around, but I console myself with the thought that I can easily outrun him.

'You don't need to worry about Jonty,' Melanie Smithson chatters on. 'He'll probably have forgotten about it by tomorrow.'

Yeah, right! Harrison will tell Jonty, and they'll be on my case tomorrow.

Why me? What have I ever done?

My stomach is churning; it's like my insides are turning somersaults. I feel sick and won't be in tomorrow, I'm sure.

FIVE

I'm trying to put the other day out of my mind.

Jonty probably bunked off school today just to avoid the history test.

My feet feel heavy as I drag myself towards Mr Jones' classroom this afternoon.

My heart is racing. I fear it will explode. I need to take big, deep breaths.

I'm sure Harrison is trimming his knuckles and looking to find a nice, quiet spot in the playground where he can remind me of the previous day's conversation.

I really hope Mr Jones is already here. I've timed my entry to exactly one minute before half-past.

At least it should postpone any confrontation.

My stomach is straining, the knots getting tighter, as I hover outside the classroom.

I can see through the gap around the edge of the

door, and breathe a sigh of relief as I spy a suited figure moving towards his desk.

Mr Jones is here.

Mole raises his head slightly above the parapet. It's all clear.

I start to relax, and move quietly towards my usual seat. Melanie Smithson and Ben Gillet are chatting away animatedly.

I search round the rest of the room but can't see Jonty.

Mr Jones starts the afternoon register.

Harrison is sitting at his desk alone, and as I glance at him, I notice his spotty complexion. I hadn't observed that before. He's not jumping all over the place, acting as though he's eaten bags of sugar for breakfast, performing his usual routine before Jonty grabs his nose and gives it a tweak.

Harrison hasn't even noticed me.

I'm mulling this over when Melanie Smithson suddenly spins round.

'Have you heard?'

'Heard what?' I ask.

'Told you Jonty wouldn't bother you again.' She smiles.

'Why, where is he?' I say, trying to hide the panic in my voice.

'Harrison said he didn't come home last night.'

'You said he would probably forget all about it,' I correct her.

I glance over to where Harrison is sitting to make sure he isn't listening.

'It's the same thing, isn't it?' she says.

A face full of freckles leans across. 'I mean, he's not here, is he?' Ben Gillet adds.

I force a smile, but it feels false and actually hurts my face. I can't understand why Jonty's mouth doesn't hurt when he grins so much.

I try and work out what Ben Gillet means. I have to factor in that Ben Gillet is the sort of boy who always speaks before engaging his brain.

'He's probably staying at a friend's house,' I suggest.

'Harrison said his mum has called the police,' says Melanie Smithson.

'Police?' I repeat, alarmed.

Mr Jones runs through the register, and the only one missing is Jonty.

'Probably caught the train to London, or something,' suggests Ben Gillet.

His eyes are open wide, as though he's completely certain he's figured it out.

Melanie Smithson doesn't even wait to give merit to Ben's suggestion.

'I think they would have checked that, don't you?' she says, her voice clipped.

Ben Gillet's confidence nosedives.

'They'll have covered stations, buses, all that,' says Melanie Smithson dismissively.

I feel slightly relieved, and sense my muscles half relaxing.

Jonty still hasn't arrived.

'Police will check the local area, garden sheds, treehouses, that sort of thing,' Melanie Smithson adds with authority.

Ben Gillet nods. 'Mmm, hadn't thought of that.'

'He might have had an accident,' I say.

'Think the hospital would have been in touch,' retorts Melanie Smithson.

Still, the thought of Jonty not being at school isn't the worst news.

Yesterday's history test results still rankle, so I bury my head in my school bag and rearrange some of my textbooks.

Melanie Smithson thinks she knows everything.

The most obvious result of Jonty's non-appearance this morning is that I can now see all the playing fields, without Jonty's wide frame obstructing the view. He tends to block out part of the soccer pitch, and I can now watch games lessons without having to bob and weave around his large head.

'Actually, you were probably one of the last people to see Jonty.' Melanie Smithson's index finger flicks in my direction.

She doesn't know everything, and I'm not going to tell her.

'You saw him as well,' I counter.

The thought of the police talking to me makes me shaky. I wonder what they'd want to know.

'You're both witnesses!' Ben Gillet's eyes nearly leave their sockets.

That's not good.

I'm surprised Harrison hasn't paid any attention to me this morning, although he's not missing Jonty that much, as he violently rocks sideways on his chair, trying to knock Abi Linton off her seat.

'The police will want a statement from you.' Ben Gillet is already in the court-room and filing the newspaper headline.

'Jonty will be in tomorrow as usual,' I say with little conviction.

I daren't get my hopes up too much that Jonty has more pressing issues to deal with, other than my face.

*

Uncle Steven is sitting in his wheelchair by the fire when I arrive home from school.

His eyes light up when he sees me. I rush over to him and hug him. He holds me tightly with his good arm and squeezes me. He growls like a bear, before letting me go.

'How you doing, my man?' he asks. His face seems fuller, probably because he doesn't get out of his wheelchair often to move about.

'Yeah, all right, thanks.' I smile. 'How long are you staying?'

He visits a lot more now, as Mum says he isn't managing very well at his house.

'Not sure, probably till next Wednesday. That's if

I don't drive your mum mental,' he says, and pulls a face.

'I heard that,' shouts Mum through the kitchen.

Uncle Steven works at the independent school at the top of the hill outside town. He's on some advisory board that discusses disability issues. I bet he's really good at his job.

'Looks like we've also got the boys in blue looking after us,' he quips. 'Two police cars are at the end of the street. Special protection for special people, I reckon,' he says, whispering behind his hand.

Mum and Uncle Steven couldn't be less alike. He's always cheerful, which I don't really get, because he can't do the stuff most people can.

'Yeah, I saw them on my way home.' I try to sound casual.

Mum is writing a note to herself as she comes through to the lounge.

The table smells of disinfectant. Table mats and cutlery are laid out for the sacred hour of five.

'I was starting to get worried,' Mum says.

I let out a deep sigh in the direction of Uncle Steven. Mum is always fussing.

'I'm always home at this time. What's so different about today?'

'Haven't you heard?'

'Jonty?' I casually ask.

'Is that his name? I don't remember the police calling him that... but I suppose it's his nickname.'

'The police are at the end of the street. Are they knocking on doors?' I try to keep my voice calm.

'Has anyone given you a nickname, Michael? I used to get called "Debs" – because of Deborah, I suppose. Quite liked it actually...'

'Mum never called you Debs,' dismisses Uncle Steven. 'It was always Deborah,' he pronounces, in a posh voice.

'She hardly ever called me by my name, let alone a nickname,' Mum says, glaring.

Uncle Steven draws in his cheeks and waits for the moment to pass.

I could see Mum drifting off to some faraway place, way back in time.

'I had lots of friends when I was younger,' she adds.

Uncle Steven raises his eyebrows but says nothing.

'The police, did they come here?' I prompt her.

'Yes, they did, and I had no idea what they were talking about. They said he's in your class.'

My throat goes dry.

'They must have taken the school register and gone to the houses of everyone in your class.'

'What time did they say he went missing?' I ask.

'From the time he left school yesterday. Did you see him?'

'I saw him in class but not to talk to.' I can feel my voice faltering. I cough to clear my throat. 'Umm, I've got some homework to do, so I'll be in my room.'

'Aw, c'mon, Sherlock, you must have some clues,' persists Uncle Steven.

He tries to move forward and grab me, but lurches back involuntarily in his chair.

'You okay, Uncle Steven?' I say, alarmed, as he fights to regain control.

I watch him flinch slightly as his head lurches back in a swift movement.

'Course,' he says, looking straight at me. 'Now,' he moves his fingers across his jaw, 'if it's reward money you're after, I could run to a pound perhaps, for any classified information.'

He presses a coin into my hand.

I hesitate for a second, before getting the joke.

Mum looks worried.

'Anything else happen today, Michael?' she says quickly. 'Anyone you got chatting to?' I can see a gleam in her eye, as though the rest of her day depends on my answer.

'Not really.'

'So do you know him very well?'

'If you mean Jonty, no, I don't know him very well. Why should I?' I hear my voice strain.

My shoulders instinctively hunch as I remember his stale breath seeping into my pores, his face pushing up against mine.

'Bit odd, isn't it? They say he never went home last night,' Mum says.

I shrug. I can sense Mum's in the mood to push for answers, and I don't want to talk.

'Interrogation over, sir, but don't leave the country. Just in case we want to talk to you again,' says Uncle

Steven, in a serious gruff voice.

I smile towards Uncle Steven, before leaving for my room.

'Oh, Nana's coming to dinner on Sunday,' Mum shouts up the stairs. 'Expect she'll want to see Uncle Steven, and you too, Michael,' she quickly adds, with little enthusiasm. 'You haven't seen her in a while.'

Not looking forward to that. There's always a bit of tension in the air when Nana comes.

She hasn't been to visit us in our new house yet.

I throw myself on the bed but feel uneasy; I'm half expecting the police to knock again at the door.

I'm being honest. I *didn't* speak to Jonty. Not really. It was more like the Spanish Inquisition. That's not what I call a real conversation.

We never even got to speak in the woods. What was I supposed to do?

The thought of his big, flabby arm against my throat gives me goosebumps.

He'll turn up tomorrow all right.

I am already trying to plan my day so as to avoid him.

Registration is safe enough because we're all together. I can slip off to the library at break and keep a lookout for him from there, especially if it's a fine day. I'll go to the late sitting at lunchtime because Jonty likes to go to the first one. That just leaves home time… which could be a problem.

Keep your head down, Mole.

SIX

Wednesday morning.
So far so good.

No sign of Jonty at the moment, although Harrison and Pierce are walking ahead of me, heads bowed and chatting.

This time, there's none of their usual behaviour: shoving and pulling each other's coats, until one of them falls into a garden, or gets pushed against a fence. They nearly always arrive with their trousers grubbed up, and their jackets sullied, but today they're just walking.

As I turn the final corner, I stop in my tracks. Melanie Smithson is talking to a police officer at the bottom of the steps leading to the school hall.

He's nodding and making notes.

I cross the driveway and try to walk sideways up the

thirty or so steps towards the hall, so Melanie Smithson doesn't see me.

I lift one half of my jacket and bury my face in it, pretending to look for a pen or something.

I get strange looks from a couple of Year Sevens, who are watching me negotiate the steps like a crab.

I glance towards Melanie Smithson. She's got a half-smile on her face. She's acting as though she's just solved one of the biggest mysteries ever.

She is *so* annoying.

I breeze past, pretending not to notice. But my plan is thwarted as she runs up the steps and catches me up.

'I think I've given him some valuable information, wouldn't you know.' She throws her head back and pulls her books closer to her chest.

'What information?'

'I told him what I saw.'

I shrug my shoulders, trying to appear disinterested, but I really want to know.

Melanie Smithson is the most annoying person I've ever met.

'I know Jonty picks on you. And Harrison was giving you a hard time after Mr Logie's lesson.'

'What?'

'That's right. I came to your rescue, remember?'

'I didn't need rescuing,' I mumble.

I start to feel all hot and bothered under my clean collar.

'Harrison was threatening you.'

'We were just talking,' I say in exasperation.

'Didn't sound like it to me. You were trapped, like a rabbit in headlights.'

I want to say *more like a mole*.

'I would have been all right.'

'Huh, he'd have you for breakfast, Michael Dobson, and you know it.' She glares at me, defying me to disagree. 'Anyway, I told the police what I heard, so they'll want to talk to you.'

'What can I tell them, if you've told them everything?'

'Dunno. I didn't get there till it looked like you'd ordered a knuckle sandwich. I've got no idea what happened before then. Anyway, you were one of the last people to see Jonty.'

'So?'

'So!' Melanie Smithson folds her arms and leans forward.

I screw my eyes up and move slightly backwards, as she tilts her face perilously close to me.

She is *so irritating*.

I feel 'Mole' disappearing underground, keeping his head down till all this has blown over. I just know Melanie Smithson is enjoying having the spotlight firmly on her.

All I can think of is Jonty and Harrison setting their sights on me, once this mess is sorted out. Jonty still has unfinished business with me.

'None of us know for sure where Jonty is,' I say quietly.

Melanie tilts her head slightly upwards. 'No, I suppose not,' her eyes slanting as though she is giving it some thought.

I feel my collar tighten. My mouth is desperately dry. I gulp air and turn away from Melanie Smithson's clutches. I walk back down the steps and over to a low wall next to the staff car park and sit down.

My head is swirling and filling up with a kind of fog, and I know I'll faint if I carry on walking.

The police want to see me? What's Mum going to think? The neighbours will start talking, and she'll get dead embarrassed.

I can hear footsteps gathering pace as students hurry to their classes for register.

My body is shaking and I take a deep breath to instil calm. Need to wait for the moment to pass.

Mole knows the signs. He knows when it's safe to peek above the ground to make sure the danger has gone.

Suddenly Mr Logie appears. He rides a bike to school. He says most people ride bikes in Amsterdam, where he used to live.

He raises an arm to signal to me he wants a word.

He pulls his briefcase out of his saddlebag.

'Everything all right, Michael?' he asks as he parks his bike. He sits next to me on the wall.

Mr Logie has black, shiny shoes with laces. His trousers are spotless, without any creases. It's as though there's a glossy sheen covering his whole body. Like an eagle.

He has an old newspaper in his hand.

'I hope our conversation yesterday didn't make you unduly worried about Spinney Wood.' He places his hand on my arm.

I freeze.

He unfolds the newspaper, which is a bit frayed, and hands it to me.

I look at the date. It's twenty-five years old.

Schoolboy goes missing in Spinney Wood.

I study the picture. The boy seems strangely familiar, but I can't explain why.

Mr Logie takes the paper back out of my hands. His face is pinched.

'A good friend of mine,' he says. He folds the newspaper, placing it in his briefcase.

His eyes glaze over. He looks sad. I avert my gaze.

'I think I'll be late for registration, sir,' I start.

But he has this faraway look, interrupted by the occasional sigh.

It's nearly register for pity's sake. I can't be late, but how do I leave?

Mr Logie opens his mouth to speak, but pauses. His beady eyes dart from side to side.

'We were a bit older than you, probably about fifteen or sixteen. Looking forward to leaving school actually...' He smiles.

I press firmly down on the floor to stop my knees from shaking.

'We did everything together,' he continues.

I guess I have to listen.

'He came from a rough estate, and didn't have it easy at home. He never complained. Never said much actually – a bit like you in that respect.' He offers me another smile. 'There was only his mother to look out for him, although she didn't do a very good job.'

Out of the corner of my eye, I can see a trickle of children scurrying to class.

Still no sign of Jonty.

'He was always bunking off school,' he adds.

Mum would definitely make a note about that.

I can't sit on this wall forever. The bell will go any minute. I could be marked late. Mum wouldn't be pleased.

My feet begin to fidget, moving tiny bits of gravel around. It's surprising how quickly you can build up a little pile of the stuff. But I suddenly stop, conscious that it might annoy Mr Logie.

I nervously watch a couple of police officers searching the sports ground. Combing for clues, I suppose. If they see me sitting here, they might want to talk to me about Jonty.

I should be getting inside.

I bet the other teachers are already in the staff room. Mr Logie probably doesn't have a lesson first thing.

'My friend used to make this den, somewhere he could spend the night. He used to build up a fire with kindling and bits of snapped-off branches. Shame about the trees, I know, but he would freeze without a bit of heat. He was amazing the way he could start a fire. The tiny flames would start to lick the wood gently, and within moments, sparks would turn into a proper blaze.'

'I'm not allowed out at night,' I say.

'I know, I know,' he says. 'Your mother said as much at parents' evening. She said you were a bit of a worrier. We had a good chat that night, if you remember.' He nods at me, as though he understands.

I can't imagine being in the freezing cold, with the wind howling; it sends shivers through my body.

'It was a bit spooky. The trees would moan all night long if the wind took hold,' Mr Logie continues.

Suddenly the groaning breath of the trees in Spinney Wood flashes through my mind.

I start to think about his friend.

I start to think about Jonty.

'One day, after school, he went to the wood to start a fire as usual and you know what? He never came back. He just… vanished.' A sad expression lines his face.

I wait a moment before speaking. 'What do you think happened to him?'

My brain is in overdrive trying to join up all the dots.

'The police couldn't explain it. It was as though he'd disappeared off the face of the earth.'

Disappeared.

'He always wanted to live abroad. Talked about living in Holland… Europe, anywhere,' he hastily adds.

I suppose the police can't explain everything.

'So you need to be careful, young Dobson. We

don't want you going missing, do we?' he says, a sad expression lining his face.

'No, sir. That's sad about your friend, sir.'

Mr Logie's back stiffens.

'Yes, it's sad beyond measure,' he says glumly.

I stand up and start to leave.

'Oh, by the way, Michael, no need to tell anyone about this conversation. You understand?' He raises his eyebrows at me.

I have this niggling feeling Mr Logie wants to tell me more about Spinney Wood, but something is stopping him.

My head is spinning. So many thoughts.

Keep your head down, Mole.

SEVEN

'**I** can't understand what's going on, Michael!' Mum's high-pitched voice rings like an alarm bell.

Great! Not even *hello, Michael, how was your day?*

Jonty Johnson's whereabouts have stumped everyone. Even Pierce came up to me and grunted, 'All right,' before catching up with Harrison and barging him into the other side of the corridor.

It was all a bit too quiet.

Till I got home.

'Are you all right? Do you think it's safe at the moment?' Mum starts to pepper me with questions.

'Where's Uncle Steven?' The lounge is empty.

'He's tired, so he's having a nap. Did you hear what I said?'

'What do you mean, safe?' I say, throwing my blazer onto the sofa.

'This Jonty who's gone missing, it's happening all over again.' She's almost shouting now. She picks up my blazer and hangs it on the coat and hat stand in the hallway.

'He's only gone missing,' I explain.

'It's happened before,' she says, and grips my arm. She pulls me slowly round the lounge, then lowers me carefully down into an armchair. She's holding my wrists in a vice-like grip.

'I've seen the news.'

'So?' I sigh, annoyed that I'm getting the full blast.

'They said that years ago another boy went missing and was never seen again. It was on the television this lunchtime.'

'Can you let go!' I snap and tug my arm away from her.

'It's happening again,' she says. 'Michael, don't you see? It's history repeating itself. A boy goes into Spinney Wood, and that's the last we hear of him. Nobody has a clue what's happened.'

History repeating itself... the words reverberate around my head.

'Spinney Wood?' I ask.

'It's here, on our doorstep. I would never have moved here if I'd known,' Mum says, throwing her head in the air.

Why would anyone check out the local woods before they move?

'Everyone is talking about it. It's on the radio, on

the television. I was on the phone with the builder this morning and he's lived round here for years. He said it's been happening more and more recently.'

Her words are just noise now in my head.

'There are probably bodies out there in Spinney Wood,' she announces.

'Bodies!' I repeat with alarm.

That's not good news.

'They're checking on other children who've gone missing over the years,' she cries.

Mr Logie's sharp beak fills my mind.

'There could be more! They're probably going to dig up Spinney Wood this week!' Mum's getting really agitated now.

I imagine row upon row of 'Jontys' buried under the massive beech trees, their long, spindly branches draped over the bodies.

What Jonty did, and where he went, isn't my problem. I feel some relief he won't be hunting me down. I should just forget about the stupid woods and Jonty Johnson.

I don't care if I never see him again.

Mum worries me more; she is breathing quite hard now.

Her hands are on my shoulders, and she's rocking me backwards and forwards.

'Mum, stop!' I shout.

'You must promise me,' she shrieks, 'never to go up there!' Her eyes blaze. 'Michael?' she cries with urgency.

'Mr Logie told me all about that other boy, the one who went missing,' I blurt.

'What?'

'Mr Logie says his friend went missing when he was a child.'

'Yes, in Spinney Wood, I expect,' shouts Mum.

There she goes, jumping to conclusions as usual.

'Mr Logie, your history teacher?'

She lets go of my shoulders and walks over to the sideboard, to reach for her notepad.

'I told you. There's something really sinister about those woods. I never liked the look of them when we went for a walk that time, do you remember? You wait till I see Mr Logie. I'll give him a piece of my mind.'

I wish I hadn't said anything. He'd asked me to keep quiet.

'It's got nothing to do with Mr Logie,' I protest.

I don't want Mr Logie to think I've said something.

Mum's eyes move sideways, as though they're frantically searching for a link between Jonty, Spinney Wood and a hidden graveyard of bodies.

'Don't raise your voice to me, I'm your mother.' She grips the notebook and stares into space.

'You don't know Mr Logie like I do,' I say calmly. 'He talks to you, properly, and he tells you things,' I say in his defence.

Mum sighs. 'I can't think straight, Michael. It's been such a stressful day with this news and everything. You wouldn't understand.'

My heart beats faster, and I feel hot. Mum seems to be locked in her own little world. She's not really listening to me.

'What can his family be thinking?' she muses, shaking her head slowly.

'There's only his mum… nobody else cares!' I say through clenched teeth.

'Well, there's only me that worries about you. Your dad's never here!' Mum snaps.

Not really true. Dad is away because of work for a couple of days sometimes.

It's a quarter to five, and Mum hasn't even started tea. I'm really hungry.

'The police say he never went home. He went straight to Spinney Wood from school. I wonder who the last person he saw was before he entered the woods. No cameras around those woods, you know.'

I lower my head. I need a glass of water. Not sure what else to say.

I feel shaky just thinking about Spinney Wood. And that last meeting with Jonty. What if he's still in there?

I leave her stewing over Spinney Wood and walk through to the kitchen to get some water.

Returning to the lounge, I see that Mum hasn't even moved. She's gone strangely quiet, her knuckles white against the notebook.

I wonder if she's all right.

I take a big swig of water, which is refreshing. My shoulders are aching with all this tension.

Mum turns her back to me; one hand is resting on the mantelpiece.

I'm sure she'll be fine in a minute, but don't think I can move until she speaks. Just to be sure.

She looks smaller, now she's stopped shouting. There are wisps of grey curled around her ears and her body seems hunched, as though she's holding herself in.

I move slightly to get a better view of her. Her hand is perilously close to the decorative farm animals on either side of the clock. One ornament has a broken gate with a sheep behind it, and I can count one, two, three sheepdogs playing.

I hope Mum doesn't knock the piece off the shelf. Her hand is trembling, and quite close to the sheep. I know she spends ages cleaning her ornaments, so she'd be really upset if it got broken.

I feel more relaxed now I'm thinking about something different. It stops me from worrying. I probably see things others don't see.

'Everything okay in there?' Uncle Steven's voice echoes through the hallway. He's sitting in his wheelchair outside his bedroom door.

'Think so,' I reply, moving into the hallway. 'Mum got a bit worked up. You know how she gets sometimes,' I say defensively.

'Hasn't changed much over the years,' Uncle Steven surmises.

'Was she a bit like me then, when she was younger?' I ask.

'Bit of a tomboy, was your mother,' he reveals.

'Really?'

'Preferred climbing trees, messing about down at the river. She even played football and started her own team.'

'So, nothing like me,' I conclude.

'She was a nightmare for your nan. Never knew what she'd get up to next. Then it all changed.' His face becomes downcast.

I am just about to ask Uncle Steven what he means, when I see Mum standing in the hallway. That's the signal for Uncle Steven to retreat into his room.

Mum forces a smile.

'I hope you never go up there, Michael,' Mum suddenly says.

Let it go…

'No chance,' I reply.

'Straight back from school tomorrow, you understand.'

'I always come straight back. Why wouldn't I?' I feel annoyed she's going on again about Spinney Wood.

'I wish your dad would speak to you. It's all work, work, work with him!' Mum snaps.

She turns and walks slowly into the kitchen.

I'm about to head for my bedroom, when there is a knock at the door.

Mum flies back from the lounge and opens the door.

It's a police officer.

She waits for what seems like ages, before ushering the constable in, and along the hallway.

She usually invites people to sit down, but we all just stand around, because we're waiting for him to speak.

'Michael, this nice police officer wants to talk to you, I expect.' Mum has her 'polite' voice on.

I'm not sure how she knows he's nice. He looks a bit young for a police officer. He has a few patches of red rash on his face. He could use lemon juice to get rid of them.

I feel my heart thumping in my chest and gulp a lungful of air. The police officer smiles, trying to put me at ease. I expect he'll say sorry for interrupting my tea. Then he'll talk about how I'm doing at school, and gradually work up to Spinney Wood.

We haven't had tea yet.

The young officer takes off his helmet and looks directly at me. I lower my head to avoid his eyes and instead stare at his shiny uniform and buttons.

'Michael, mind if I ask you a few questions?' he asks.

It's nearly five to five.

Tea will have to be put back today, but Mum doesn't seem to notice the time. Still, it's only one day.

'Michael, the police officer's talking to you,' Mum says.

I look up at Mum and then across to the police officer.

The blotches on his face seem to be even redder. I feel sorry for him. It might be eczema.

But then I think of Jonty and his huge angry face.

The police officer pulls out a notebook, and I see his pen at the ready – a bit like Mum. But this is far more important.

'Just a few questions really, it shouldn't take long. I expect you'll want your tea.'

I nod, and he flicks over a page.

'Did you speak to Jonathan Johnson in school on Monday?'

'We had a sort of chat,' I say.

'You never told me that,' says Mum.

I want to wriggle away and dive for cover. My mouth is dry, and I swallow hard.

The police officer gestures to me to continue my story, but the words seem stuck somewhere between my brain and his leather notebook.

'Michael, we're waiting,' says Mum crossly. She probably thinks I'm deliberately avoiding the question. I want to go to the toilet. I feel faint but I'll just have to stay here. I grab hold of the edge of the table as my head swims.

'I think he needs a glass of water,' the police officer says.

'What? Oh yes,' replies Mum.

She places the water in front of me, and I slowly drink, my eyes now level with the police officer's top button. I wonder if he has to clean his own uniform, or if there's a police laundry where they do it for him.

He sits there patiently while I finish my drink.

'Tell the police officer what you said to Jonathan,' urges Mum.

'He was a bit annoyed.'

'Why was that?' asks the officer.

I'm not going to say Jonty is permanently annoyed with me.

'Not sure. Suppose because he never does well in class. Like history.'

'Can you believe they have league tables in his history class, like football? In the middle of a lesson!' exclaims Mum.

'It's always at the end,' I say.

The police officer gives Mum a look to tell her to stop talking.

'Umm, it was nothing much really,' I say.

'Did you get angry?' the police officer asks.

'Michael never gets angry,' points out Mum. 'Just like to keep your head down, don't you, Michael?'

'And nothing else?' says the police officer.

It isn't my fault if Jonty's lost, or gone camping, or disappeared in Spinney Wood.

'I saw him with… someone,' I tentatively say. I avoid looking up at Mum or the police officer.

'You never said!' Mum says, shocked.

I'm glad the police officer is here for the next bit.

'I saw Jonty in Spinney Wood with this woman.' I stare straight at the police officer.

'Spinney Wood! After all I've said about staying away from there!' Mum screeches.

The police officer leans towards me. 'Did you recognise this person?' He stays a hand towards Mum, motioning for her to keep still.

'An old woman, but I didn't really get a good look at her,' I point out.

'Could you try to describe her?' he encourages me.

'She was small and had a stick. Her face was a grey colour, like she was ill.'

'Did she seem friendly?' the police officer enquires.

'They were chatting. But I didn't hear what they said. I didn't stay long,' glancing at Mum.

Leave it to the police, I silently plead with her.

But she goes off again.

'I've told him a *dozen* times not to go into Spinney Wood. Are you going to tell him?' Mum rounds on the police officer.

'I think your mother is right, Michael – until we've found Jonathan at least.' He gives me a kind smile.

'I hope he hasn't been picking on you, Michael?' Mum asks.

'I hardly know him, I told you,' I say, and screw my nose up at her.

'He's quite sensitive,' says Mum in a whisper to the police officer.

All these questions are making me anxious. I feel my stomach churn; the knots begin to tighten.

I picture Jonty, leaning over me, really angry, his contorted features warning me to keep quiet. His fist nudges up against my chin and jerks it upwards. I should keep my mouth shut.

'Not to worry, Michael. If you think of anything else, just let us know,' the police officer finally says, and closes his notebook.

'It's probably a bit much for him. He's a bit of a worrier,' Mum says.

I cringe.

I collapse into an armchair while Mum shows the police officer out. I hear them chatting in the hallway and know they're talking about me.

I shouldn't have said anything, still less about Jonty getting annoyed. He'll kill me.

EIGHT

It's all a bit weird at school at the moment.

There are a couple of police officers walking around the school grounds, and everyone tries to avoid them.

I feel safer while they're around.

They stop to chat to each other every so often, but they probably use coded words so we can't understand what they're saying.

They should be concentrating on Spinney Wood.

I head along the corridor, and away from them, into Mr Jones' classroom.

It's quieter in school now; there's no singing or shouting in the corridors. No teachers standing at the foot of the stairs, to complain about the noise.

If Harrison has told Jonty about the history test, I'll say I was clearing my throat. My airwaves do get blocked sometimes, and I have to clear them; otherwise, I get really panicky when the words get stuck.

Rehearsing what to say gives me a headache; the phrases go round and round my brain, like a hamster on a wheel.

I see Melanie Smithson and Ben Gillet ahead, and duck my head so they don't see me.

There's nothing I should be worried about, and Harrison has already filed into Mr Jones' classroom. I see his bulky frame ahead of me turn into the room.

Keep going and pretend everything's okay. I'm like everyone else who hasn't seen Jonty for two days.

'Michael, have they spoken to you yet?'

Melanie Smithson tilts her head to one side, like a grown-up expecting an answer.

I like her saying my name. It gives me a warm, fuzzy feeling.

I kind of like Ben too. He's a bit of a fruit cake, but harmless, I think.

'They came to the house,' I tell her.

We've stopped outside the classroom.

'Is he here?' I ask. I rock from side to side nervously.

'No,' replies Melanie, and says nothing else.

A faint smile lights up my face. I can relax for the rest of the day.

'Well?' Melanie prompts. 'Did the police speak to you?'

I feel like it's me under investigation the way she asks questions. All official, making a mental note of things.

'I couldn't tell them anything,' I say. 'Not sure why they're still here. They should be searching Spinney Wood.'

I shrug my shoulders and hope that's got her off my back.

Melanie and Ben lower their heads conspiratorially.

'I agree,' Melanie says. 'It makes no sense, hanging around here. They've searched everywhere.'

I pause, wondering if she expects me to respond.

Ben pipes up. 'You can't hide a body in a school anyway, although the playground should be double-checked.'

'You can *see* the playground, dummy. What *can't* you see?' asks Melanie.

'But what about *under* the playground?' Ben wags his finger, emphasising the word *under*. 'Concrete can be dug up, and bodies stashed there.'

'I think someone might have heard a digger at night, don't you?' Melanie gives Ben a withering look.

'Gangs do that all the time in London, under motorways, and even under churches,' Ben enthuses.

I'm not sure if Ben is serious, or if he's seen too many gangster films.

'I expect the police are still here, in case someone remembers something,' Melanie says, ignoring Ben.

'We just need to forget it,' I say.

'On the other hand, you wouldn't be able to smell a rotting body if it was hidden in Spinney Wood. There's all sorts of different smells in there. It could be years before they found it... unless maybe a dog, or something, digs up the bones,' says Ben, who seems to be getting more imaginative by the minute.

'And it's happened before in Spinney Wood,' Melanie says, nodding thoughtfully.

'Is that right?' A tall, poker-faced police officer stands over us. 'Did Johnson say he was going up there when you spoke to him?' he asks.

'Not to me he didn't,' I gulp, convinced I should say something about what really happened that afternoon.

'Do you think that's where he disappeared?' asks Melanie.

'We're following all lines of enquiry. It is a missing person's enquiry and nothing more,' the officer says, his face expressionless.

'He's probably collapsed and fallen down a hole,' says Ben.

I catch Melanie rolling her eyes.

'We're not ruling anything out,' the police officer replies, although the look on his face suggests he is ruling that out.

But Ben is not letting go of his latest theory. 'He can always suck on leaves if he gets dehydrated,' adds Ben.

'That's stupid,' says Melanie.

'Commandos do that as part of their survival techniques,' Ben says knowledgeably.

'As I said, it's a missing person investigation.' The officer gives Ben a look of disdain before turning to Melanie. 'And yes, we are concentrating our search in Spinney Wood.'

'As we've said before, if you think of anything else

that might be relevant, let me know. I'll be around the school for the next day or so.' The officer strides off past the main reception, and heads outside.

'We need to pay Spinney Wood a visit,' says Melanie.

'We?' I say. 'I can't go.'

'Don't you want to know what's happened to Jonty?' she accuses.

'We could send a drone up… you know? Like we're on some sort of spy mission,' says Ben with enthusiasm.

Melanie frowns.

I just want to get into Mr Jones' classroom.

I'm wondering how long it will be before Jonty catches up to me, grabs me and grips me in a headlock. I imagine him pummelling away at my bloodied face, until he's taught me a lesson.

We go into the classroom and I quickly scan the room. Jonty's seat is vacant, and Harrison and Pierce are slumped against the backs of their chairs, waiting for the register to be called.

Their faces are pensive, which isn't like them one little bit. I don't think either of them has had a deep thought. Ever.

A low murmur of chatter circulates the room. It stops immediately when Mr Jones starts to talk.

'I know it's very difficult for you, for everyone at the moment, what with the police here. And we all want to find some answers. I want to let you know that there is someone available for you to talk to here at school, if you feel that would help.'

You can hear a pin drop.

He begins to call the register. He skips Jonty Johnson's name.

*

Double maths.

I don't actually mind maths as it's just a question of getting it right. Or wrong.

But the point is, you can't have bits in between. Like putting your hand up, and offering reasons why this, or that, could be helpful. It's logic. Right or wrong. Simple as that.

So I get my head down and concentrate on the problems on the page, rather than inside my head.

But an image of Jonty's oversized face creeps above the paper, his chubby hands grabbing the ruled lines and pulling them apart.

Soon he's filled the textbook and spread himself across the algebra, hiding in the numbers. Especially the number eight. His bulging eyes are staring right at me in the top circle, and his enormous gaping mouth is in the bottom circle.

Soon, he's moving closer, climbing off the page and into my face.

His teeth are sharp and jagged, filled with bits of food. His mouth is like a mammoth cave. Pitch-black, and I can't see where it ends. I'm getting sucked into the black hole, and I'll disappear forever.

I can't think straight. He's coming for me. A smirk covers his face. I'm sinking, and know I'll just be swallowed up.

I try and press my hands against the desk to stop myself from falling into Jonty's mouth. His bad breath is hot and sticky, and makes me feel drowsy, and it's only a matter of time before—

'Everything all right, Dobson?' The bearded face of Mr Yates, the maths teacher, is speaking.

'What?' I croak.

'Do you want some water?' he asks.

'Oh no, I'm fine, sir.' I glance round to see if anyone is watching me, but most of them have their heads down.

Mr Yates waits over me for a few seconds to make sure I'm all right.

I adjust my seat, pulling myself upright, and fix my eyes on the maths question again.

*

After maths has finished, I spy Mr Logie in the corridor.

He's making sure that the flow of students is going the right way. One side is heading for the canteen. The other line is going to the games field.

I'm not really hungry.

I've got loads of questions, lining up one behind the other. But they're questions I can't get straight or know how to ask.

I slowly walk up to where Mr Logie is directing the traffic.

Wait patiently until he turns round.

'Michael? What is it?' he says, surprised to see me.

'Sorry, sir, have you got a minute?' I ask.

He gives a deep sigh, before ushering me into his classroom.

I lean against the sky-blue wall. There's a map on the wall, with a timeline showing the different ages. It goes right back to the pre-historic period.

I'm sure Mr Logie won't mind me asking a few questions. I rub the tops of my fingers one against the other; it calms me.

'Well, what is it? It's lunchtime,' he points out, setting his briefcase on the desk.

'Did they find anything else in Spinney Wood?' I begin. 'Anything that was from ages ago?'

'You really are interested, aren't you?' he says. But I can see he's slightly twitchy, his fingers twiddling with the lock on his briefcase.

'A little,' he says. 'Over the years, there have been digs that unearthed artefacts, such as knives and eating implements, which they could date back to the Neolithic period.'

'So there was nothing they said about a mystery woman then?' I ask tentatively.

He eyes me with suspicion. 'A mystery woman?' He chuckles, but his voice falters slightly.

'Be careful, Michael,' he suddenly cautions. His face

becomes hard.

'Careful?' I ask.

'Well, Spinney Wood has quite a history, as you know. It's best to leave things in the past well alone.'

That's an odd thing for a history teacher to say.

And I never saw the old woman *properly*. Not really.

I'm back inside my head. I picture Jonty sitting in a hollowed-out dell, surrounded by huge beech trees. Eating a burger with the chief's daughter.

His body is expanding like an inflatable balloon, before it slowly floats above the trees. He's now sitting on top of the trees, like a king on a throne. He spots me and starts to lick his lips. He wipes his mouth, which is smeared with tomato sauce.

I try to run, but my legs are concrete. Jonty leers at my feeble attempt to escape his clutches. Soon, he's taking giant strides towards me, and his unsmiling face is getting nearer.

So, still having a laugh at my expense, Dobbin? he bellows, and I start to shake uncontrollably, before closing my eyes.

'Is that all, Michael?' Mr Logie asks, raising his eyebrows.

I blink hard and exhale slowly. 'Yes, thanks, sir. I hope Jonty shows up soon,' I lie.

Mr Logie gives an odd smile, drawing in his gums. His eagle's head swivels sharply, and his cold eyes grip me.

'I shouldn't hold your breath,' is all he says.

NINE

The police finally leave Longfields, and school feels more normal. Everyone seems to be getting used to the idea that Jonty is no longer in lessons.

I don't feel jumpy anymore, walking up the school steps and through the hall. I join the students making their way to classrooms.

I'm more comfortable around the excited, loud voices that echo along the corridor. I don't even mind the occasional raucous cheer that goes up when a scuffle breaks out and I have to dodge the bags being thrown around.

Melanie and Ben are standing in the corridor, waiting for me. Melanie has her hands on her hips as if she means business.

'We need to visit Spinney Wood.'

'We can't do anything,' I protest. 'Anyway, it's not safe – the police are investigating other children who might have disappeared in Spinney Wood over the years. Kids who were never seen again!' I can feel the pitch of my voice rise… reminiscent of Mum, to my horror.

'There are three of us. Safety in numbers,' Ben points out.

'Harrison said Jonty had gone up there the night he vanished.' Melanie has that one-hundred-per-cent-I'm-right look on her face.

'Harrison doesn't know anything,' I respond.

'Oh, and *you* do, I suppose?' says Melanie.

'We need to look for clues – like a branch deliberately snapped off, or bits of thread from a coat,' says Ben.

'Even if we find anything like that, it doesn't mean he's still in Spinney Wood,' I say, feeling uncomfortable with this line of thought.

'Then where else could he be?' asks Ben. 'We know he went in, but we don't know he came out.' He taps his nose, to prove he's on the right track.

'Still, I think we need to start in Spinney Wood. We know it better than the police, so that gives us an edge,' adds Melanie.

'I hardly know it,' I complain. 'Anyway, it's got a history. You've seen the news.'

I bite my lip, knowing nothing I say will stop Melanie from wanting to visit Spinney Wood.

Ben is still focussed on the idea of finding clues.

'He might have left footprints. He's got size nines – you can hardly miss them – and it's been raining for the last few days, so the earth will be soft. There may be drops of blood that they've missed.' He's sounding a bit too enthusiastic about this for my liking.

'I know!' and Ben suddenly jerks upright. 'I just thought, I could bring Jasper,' he says excitedly.

'Who's Jasper?' I ask.

'Our dog. He's a cocker spaniel. He's great for sniffing out things.'

'He's got arthritis. He'd slow us up,' Melanie points out.

'He can still smell a rabbit at fifty paces,' Ben replies. 'Anyway, it'll give me an excuse to go to the woods. My mum's not keen on me going up there.'

'Why's that?' I ask, although I can already hear Mum's answer, shouting inside my head.

'She was talking to Abi Linton's mum, who's lived round here for years. She said weird things have happened up there,' offers Ben.

Melanie frowns. 'Like what?'

'Like another boy who went missing, when Abi's mother was at school round here,' says Ben.

'I know about him,' I say, nodding. 'Mr Logie showed me an article about him from a newspaper from years ago.'

'So why has old Logie kept an old newspaper?' Melanie asks.

'It was his friend. They used to hang out together,' I reason.

'So why are you getting a private viewing?' asks Melanie.

'Not sure,' I reply.

Melanie gives a look which says, *aren't you the lucky one!*

'My mum said it's happened more recently. She said more children have gone missing in Spinney Wood since then,' Melanie says.

'I know. It's been on the news,' I say glumly.

'It's like there's a *child catcher*!' Ben's arms start to swirl above his head while making ghostly noises.

Melanie shakes her head in despair.

Ben suddenly grabs Melanie by the shoulders. 'So let's go and visit the woods. We might see the *child catcher*,' he says in a spooky voice.

'Behave!' Melanie brushes Ben off.

I picture the trees thrashing about.

'We'll be safe. There's three of us,' reasons Melanie.

'Suppose,' I say, resigned.

'That's right,' says Ben, nodding his head and flinging his hands in the air. 'Expect the unexpected. That's what commandos do. Keep your eyes peeled.'

'What?' I say, alarmed at the mention of eyes.

'The *child catcher* could be hiding at the top of some huge tree, with a massive net they throw over children,' Ben says, and stands open-mouthed. I can tell he's picturing it.

Melanie raises her eyebrows, not impressed.

Maybe the trees are guarding secrets. A secret I know about. A secret Jonty knows about.

We all move into the classroom.

If I close my eyes, I can see the creepy trees stooping down and scooping up Jonty with their long, thick branches. They catapult him high over the town, and he's flying through the air, his arms and legs thrashing about. He lands in the canal nearby, with an almighty splash, and gallons of water soak the nearby allotments.

But wait. Jonty rises out of the murky water, like Triton or some sea god, and lands feet first on the towpath, arms crossed against his chest, head proudly aloft!

He's invincible even in my worst nightmares.

Melanie sits beside me and leans across.

'I know Ben's a bit crazy but he's right. We have to go to Spinney Wood.'

Her face is a centimetre away from my nose. I keep perfectly still so we don't accidentally touch. She's staring at me. I pull away slowly, so she doesn't think I'm being rude. I mull over what she's saying.

I don't know what it is with Melanie, but she just never gives up. And she seems to think she's right about nearly everything. I'm hoping that she'll turn round and start talking to Ben, and I can forget about Spinney Wood and never hear about it again. After all, it's just a stupid wood!

Instead, she cocks her head to one side and waits. I can sit here and ignore her and pretend she doesn't exist, but I feel my insides being prodded, and pulled and poked, until they spill out.

She is so irritating.

'What can we find that the police can't?' I whisper.

'Not sure,' she ponders, 'but at least we can check it out. So it's agreed then. Tonight, Spinney Wood, after school. We'll go to the end of the shopping precinct and work our way through to the long track at the back of Jameson Farm,' she announces.

Ben bounces about on his chair.

'I can pick up a compass and water.' His mouth is beginning to salivate with excitement.

He makes it sound like we're going on some route march through a swampy jungle, complete with dangerous predators.

It's just Spinney Wood.

'You all right with that, Michael?' asks Melanie.

Melanie's voice fades and all I can hear is Mum's impassioned instructions to stay away from Spinney Wood.

'Suppose I could say I was at one of the after-school clubs.' And just like that, Jack Flash steps out in front of Mole and I feel a sudden adrenalin rush, blocking any need for explanations.

Melony Magic, Great Goliath and Wizard's Troops are on the move!

TEN

The precinct at the top of the street has a chip shop, a fruit and vegetable store, a laundrette, a hardware shop and a space for a community hub.

I suppose it's a place for people to stop and chat, catch up with all the gossip, and talk about the weather, and the government. They do a bit of shopping and sometimes catch the bus, to take them into town.

Beyond the precinct, no more than two hundred yards away from the chippy, is the start of Spinney Wood. A well-trodden winding path leads into a small clearing surrounded by bushes and smaller trees.

Spinney Wood.

I sway backwards and forwards as I wait inside one of the small alcoves between the different shops. Glad we're going together.

Ben quickly went home to change and is now wearing his combat jacket. He looks like he's about to go over the trenches in some war movie. He seems pumped, and I imagine him as the hero, screaming at the top of his voice, running at the enemy, a bayonet fixed to his fountain pen.

However, right now he's playing with a compass he's brought, and clearly doesn't have a clue what he's doing, twisting the outer bit over and over. He spins around several times before nearly falling over.

Jasper is doing his own search, sniffing at the discarded rubbish near the bins. Orange peel and a few chips and sweet wrappers litter the ground, and he's busy licking the remnants of a fizzy drink as it runs into the drain.

Melanie comes out of the chippy and offers us some of her chips.

I hesitate, not sure if Ben should have first pick, but she thrusts the newspaper under my nose. My fingers hover over the chip paper and then I take one. Ben grabs a handful, stuffing them all in his mouth, before realising they are still piping hot!

'Serves you right,' says Melanie.

I can't help smiling.

'C'mon, let's get started,' she commands.

She strides out in the direction of Spinney Wood, and I look across at Ben, who has a steely glare on his face, which either means his mouth is sore, or he's officially on manoeuvres.

I look sideways at the dwindling numbers of people leaving the shops, and hope I'm not recognised. If Mum finds out I was in Spinney Wood, it will be the Spanish Inquisition all over again.

I need to be back by five o'clock.

We leave the shops behind, and the huge wood looms ahead. I half expect to see some blue and white ticker tape cordoning off the entrance.

It'll be better if Melanie and Ben see Jonty. I'll just show them where I saw him. Yes, that's what I'll do. Got it covered.

Things will work out all right after all.

Melanie strides out confidently, indicating she's definitely in charge and actually knows what she's doing. She is totally pathetic, considering she doesn't know where Jonty is.

The tall beech trees hover in the distance, spread out like sentries guarding an age-old secret. My skin feels clammy and cold, and there's a chill in the air.

The narrow dirt track which signals the start of the wood is loosely covered with twigs, and overgrown in places. Suddenly Melanie halts. Ben's head bumps into her back, as he's busy shaking his compass and not looking up.

'Oi! What you stopped for?' he bursts out.

'I need to get my bearings. This is a huge wood, more like a forest, and we've only got an hour before the light fades. We don't want to get lost, do we?' She fixes her gaze on Ben's compass to emphasise her point.

I slowly peer up at the trees. They stand perfectly still. It's as though they're holding their heads high and looking away.

'Here, we need to go this way,' I announce. Brushing past Ben and Melanie, I take the lead and forge ahead.

Melanie looks mildly surprised as I move forward.

I purse my lips, start to whistle, hoping it will calm my nerves. But the gathering wind catches my breath and forces me to stop.

We move silently in single file, winding our way through the copper-coloured leaves.

'Wait!' Ben shouts.

Jasper mooches over to where Ben is crouching. The dog sniffs at a brown leather belt that lies almost concealed amidst a small shrub.

'I bet this belongs to Jonty!' Ben exclaims.

'Too small,' declares Melanie, and swats Ben's suggestion away.

I nod in agreement.

After a couple of minutes, the wood forms a kind of canopy, and the sky begins to disappear.

I'll act surprised when I show them where Jonty is. Best to have them around, when we find him. He'll want to wring my neck.

It's eerily quiet as I brush past more undergrowth; the huge trees seem to be moving backwards and forwards slowly, as if they can't make their minds up. It's like they're spying to see who goes in and out.

I feel very small. Especially here among all these trees.

The track seems to get narrower and is less easy to follow.

I should have come on my own.

The occasional crunch of dry twigs and the swish of bracken are the only sounds underfoot, as we continue marching deep into the wood.

I'm sure I didn't go this far into Spinney Wood last time.

'Are we going to go much further? Time's getting on,' I say, and hope they don't notice the note of anxiety in my voice.

'If we can just cover this part, towards the quarry, that means we don't need to come back to this part of the wood again,' says Melanie.

'So we're coming back *again*?' I ask.

'The woods are huge and we'll never complete it in one go,' says Ben. 'Perhaps we should come on Saturday when we've more time.'

Melanie nods slowly. 'You okay with that, Michael?' she says.

I feel trapped, like a rabbit in headlights. My mouth is dry and I want a drink. I want a drink *at home*. But I had said I'd be an hour. Mum will have to lump it. She doesn't need to know.

Jack Flash needs to stay strong.

I'll show Melanie and Ben.

It's starting to get a little cold.

I haven't given much thought to what I'll say to Jonty

if we find him. But at least Melanie is here. She'll know what to say to him.

Anyway, as much as I can't stand Melanie with her airs and graces, she does listen. Seems to notice I have something to say.

We suddenly halt. A mass of tangled undergrowth with nettles and briars bars our way.

We're here – I think.

I signal to Melanie and Ben to wait while I investigate. I'll take it from here. Jack Flash has found a bit of courage.

I catch sight of a line of huge, golden, shimmering beeches that appear to the right. Their lower branches are twisted into a spiral curve, forming an archway. Like a magical cavern. The leaves glitter in the half-fading light, and stop me in my tracks.

The ground is throbbing, getting louder as I get closer. The same as before!

It's then that I see them.

I peer through the glistening foliage, and meet a pair of eyes staring back from among the trees. They seem to be studying me. I stay rooted to the spot, as the outline of a shadowy shape gently sways through the dense undergrowth.

A wave of panic rushes through my body and my legs start to wobble. I can't move and wish Melanie would say something. We're here. I've found it! But Ben and Melanie are still looking straight ahead, and don't seem to notice the magical archway.

The eyes hold me. They seem sad, and yet I can't look away.

I shift my head sideways to get a better look through the foliage and glimpse a mass of matted, unkempt hair that falls over the front of a weather-beaten face.

But it's the eyes that intrigue me.

I take a few steps towards them.

The humming sound gets louder the closer I get. There's a sort of energy pulsating around me.

Suddenly Jasper starts to bark. He races ahead of Ben and bursts through the undergrowth towards the base of one of the trunks, near the archway. His yelps become a frenzied howling. He tentatively moves towards the face in the bush, but then backs off, as if afraid.

'What is it, boy?' Ben shouts, racing over to comfort his dog. Jasper's moving backwards and forwards rapidly.

'He's been spooked,' says Ben.

'By what?' asks Melanie, catching up.

I turn to see Ben holding the dog tightly, and can guess what's spooked him.

My throat is dry and my tongue is stuck to my mouth. I try and force some words out, but it's impossible.

Melanie is trying to make sense of it all. 'Probably another dog,' she says at last.

Another figure suddenly appears to our right, moving stealthily through the woods. Twigs and branches are broken underfoot, alerting us of their presence.

Whoever it is, they seem to be in a hurry. All I can see is a blur passing between the branches.

But then another dog appears by our side, and the figure is forced to take a detour onto our path.

A bobble hat covers much of his face, but the beak is unmistakable.

Mr Logie is taken aback as he sees us.

'Oh, what are you all doing here?' he says. He doesn't seem too pleased.

'Exploring the woods, sir,' I reply.

'I told you it's not safe for children here,' he says.

He shuffles around; he seems nervous.

He goes over to his dog, who is sniffing about in a mass of unwieldy undergrowth – tangled bushes with short, sharp spikes block the pathway. There are thistles and prickly thorns behind them.

Melanie and Ben crouch low, peering through the mass of shrubbery.

Mr Logie tries to pull the dog away, but she remains rooted to the spot, trying to find a way underneath the tangled mass.

'C'mon, you stupid dog! Time to go!' He strains at her collar to drag her away.

Growling, the dog digs her paws into the sodden earth and refuses to budge.

'I haven't got all day, Jess. I'm warning you.'

The dog's back is arched, and her tail is stiff like a broom handle. The fur on her back is standing on edge. She's visibly agitated.

Mr Logie stands up to stretch his back when his expression suddenly changes.

His anger disappears. His lip turns upwards, as though he's just seen something that has disturbed him.

He shoots a quick look at all of us.

'Please, all of you leave right now. Go home!' he shouts. He's almost panicking.

'But we're only going for a walk, sir,' explains Melanie. She holds her arms out wide.

Mr Logie now looks very angry.

He fixes all of us with a steely gaze. 'Just go, your parents will be worried,' he snaps.

Quietly, we all turn around and make our way silently back home.

Not a word between us until we're well clear.

I glance over my shoulder. Mr Logie is watching us.

He's not going to be very pleased with us tomorrow.

ELEVEN

'You're just in time for tea, Michael. It's your favourite, fish fingers and chips,' calls Mum.

Uncle Steven is in the lounge, sitting in his wheelchair by the window.

'How's my favourite nephew?' he says, throwing his arms around me.

'Your *only* nephew,' I smile. 'Good,' I say. 'How are you?'

'Can't complain. Even if I did, no one would listen anyway,' he says, a huge grin lighting up his face.

That's what I like about Uncle Steven. He's always easy-going. Never complains.

Mum says he struggles with things like getting dressed and washing. He should think about getting some help. I love it when he comes to our house. He usually stays three or four days and then heads back to his own place. He always makes time to listen when I want to talk.

'So…what you been up to?' he begins.

I can hear Mum in the kitchen.

'Oh, the usual stuff,' I say. I throw my bag on the sofa.

'How's school?' he asks.

'Okay, I guess. I like history. The history teacher is really nice,' I say, enthused. 'We're all in teams and we have these league tables, like in football. Then we have a mini-test each week, and your team goes up or down depending on the result.'

'Ace! I think my side would have won the league. I was always a bit of a whizz at history,' he says with a knowing smile.

I grin back at him.

'Made any friends?' he asks.

'Well…' I hesitate. 'There are two people in my class who I like.'

I can hear Mum in the kitchen getting plates out of the cupboard. It won't be too long until tea.

'Tell me more, my little maestro.' Uncle Steven's eyes are wide open with expectation.

I lean closer to him. I don't want Mum to hear every word.

'There's a girl called Melanie and a boy called Ben,' I say.

I watch Uncle Steven's mind turning as he ponders this. I wait, knowing he's about to say something completely ridiculous.

'A *GIRL* called Melanie and a *BOY* called Ben.' He rolls his eyes.

'So, you *LIKE* these two kids?' He emphasises the word '*like*', drawing quotation marks in the air.

'Mmm…' I nod.

'You hang out together then?' he says, with an incredulous look on his face.

'Don't say anything to Mum, but we're looking for that lost boy,' I say.

'What, the lost boy on the news? The one who's gone missing? Tell me more, Inspector Dobson of the Yard,' he says, bowing his head in mock esteem.

He surveys my feet. 'Is that why your shoes are all muddy?'

I dart into the hallway, grab a bit of rag from the shoe rack, and give them a quick wipe.

Mum suddenly enters the lounge, armed with glove mats and hot plates.

'Here we are. You're just in time, Michael. Had a nice day?'

'Not bad,' I say.

'How was your club?' she continues.

'Club? Oh yeah, good.'

She is beaming from ear to ear as she rubs a hand on the back of my hair.

'Is it raining?' she asks, peering through the window.

'Don't think so,' I say.

I cast a pleading look at Uncle Steven, hoping he will change the direction of the conversation.

No such luck.

'Your hair's a bit wet. You don't want to catch a cold, Michael. You'll have to tell me more about this club,' Mum says, as we sit down.

Walking in Spinney Wood has made me hungry, and I devour the fish fingers and chips in no time. The tomato sauce isn't even touched.

Mum looks pleased. 'Goodness me, you were hungry. Let me get you some more.'

She disappears into the kitchen to get another packet of fish fingers out of the freezer.

'Mum doesn't like me going into Spinney Wood. You know… because of the things that have happened there,' I confide to Uncle Steven.

'I know. It's been on the telly,' he says, nodding.

'I expect it's the history club,' Mum says, returning to the lounge.

'What?'

'The club you've joined. I bet it's the history club that makes you hungry. I was the same when I joined a literary club after school. I was always famished afterwards.'

Mum sets off briskly to the kitchen to check on the fish fingers.

'So what's this history club like then? Are Melanie and Ben in the club?' Uncle Steven asks.

'Yeah,' I reply casually.

'Thought as much,' he says, tapping his nose.

'It's our history teacher who really makes the

club so good. He's pretty cool. He knows all about local history.' I pause before saying, 'He knows about Spinney Wood.'

'*Right…*' Uncle Steven says, stretching out the word, to give its full effect.

Mum comes back into the lounge balancing five fish fingers on a fish slice.

'Have you told Uncle Steven what made you join in the first place?' she asks.

'Mr Logie asked me to join, said it would be about local history.'

I hesitate, expecting her to react at Mr Logie's name, but nothing happens.

'Anyone else there, anyone you know?' she says.

'Er, no, just the three of us as usual,' I say.

That was true, but I keep my head down, staring at the empty plate.

'Oh, that's nice,' she says. She delivers the five fish fingers expertly onto my plate, and looks at me expectantly.

'So what's new about local history then?'

But it doesn't look like she's bothered about getting an answer, and she bustles back into the kitchen to do the washing-up.

I lean over to Uncle Steven and whisper, 'I know where Jonty is!'

'What, you've found him!' exclaims Uncle Steven.

I motion for him to keep his voice down.

I beam from ear to ear, and watch his eyes light up.

'I've seen him in Spinney Wood.' I nod enthusiastically.

I move even nearer but get interrupted by the noise of the front door opening.

Dad's home from work.

He spies Uncle Steven and makes a beeline for him.

Uncle Steven pauses from his meal and holds his arms out.

Dad gives him a long hug.

'How you doing, mate?' he asks Uncle Steven, at the same time patting my head affectionately.

'Can't complain…' Uncle Steven begins.

'No one would listen anyway,' Dad finishes the sentence. The two of them chuckle.

Dad brushes his hand through my hair. 'Ew!' he says, looking at his wet hand. 'Your hair's all wet. Where've you been, Michael?'

'I asked him to help with the washing-up,' interjects Uncle Steven. 'I thought his mop of hair needed a quick shampoo and wash,' he says with a wink. 'Got a bit out of hand, I'm afraid,' he adds, holding his hand up.

We're far enough away from the kitchen so Mum doesn't hear. Dad doesn't stop to check this out.

I shuffle my feet a little bit more under the table.

'Wish he'd get out more,' Dad says sharply. 'He spends far too much time in his room. Isn't that right?' he asks me pointedly.

'Well, we're all different,' says Uncle Steven, shrugging his shoulders.

'I don't like playing games much,' I explain. 'Don't know why you don't listen when I tell you that.'

'Can't get him to watch the Rovers either,' Dad says with exasperation. 'The way they're playing this season as welll!'

I watch Uncle Steven smile at Dad and then turn away. It's the first time I've seen him a bit sad.

I sometimes wonder why he's in a wheelchair. Mum hasn't told me.

Mum comes back with her own plate of dinner. She frowns at Dad. 'We don't want him playing stupid games. It's just not worth it. Anything could happen.'

'You used to play football for a girls' team when you were my age,' I say confidently.

Mum shoots a quick look towards Uncle Steven, before quickly starting to eat.

'Your dinner is in the kitchen. It needs heating up,' Mum tells Dad, without glancing up.

Dad bites his lip, forcing a smile towards Uncle Steven. 'I'll eat later.'

'C'mon, you two, eat up. You don't want it to go cold,' Mum reminds both of us.

Dad shrugs his shoulders. 'Give me a moment. I won't be a jiffy. Need to get out of these clothes,' he says, tugging at his tie before trundling upstairs to change.

'Perhaps you can invite them over, these two friends?' Mum says.

'What? No, I don't think so,' I say with surprise.

'We can make ourselves scarce, or you could all go to your room. It wouldn't be any bother.'

No *way* is that happening! I'd feel trapped, not enough space to breathe, I know I would. Anyway, I wouldn't be able to find things to talk about. What *would* we talk about? We'd run out of things to say. I might slip up and say something about the eyes.

'So, do you go anywhere else with your friends, Michael?' she says.

'They're not even friends, so there'd be no point. It's just a history club! I see them at school, that's all. I don't want to invite them, so there's no point.'

I see out of the corner of my eye that Uncle Steven is squirming in his chair.

Mole needs to escape. It's all getting too much, and Mum looks like she's gearing up for another lecture.

I feel panic rising and screw my eyes as tightly as I can to blank everything out. Mum, Melanie, Ben and the eyes. Especially the eyes.

I push my plate away, leave the table and run upstairs.

I slam my door and fling myself onto my bed. Why can't she leave me alone?

'Michael!' Mum shouts up to me.

'Go away!' I yell back.

Stupid wood! It's just a bunch of trees, for goodness' sake! It was probably the fading light and all that tangled undergrowth that made it look different. What did Melanie expect to find anyway? Who cares if Jonty Johnson is missing?

Definitely not his mum, that's for sure. I've seen her in the deputy head's office on a couple of occasions. She has her hair in a bun, and wears dangly earrings and a small ring in her nose. She speaks really loudly as well, like Jonty, like she's shouting through a megaphone. She didn't even come to parents' evening.

She won't care two hoots he's gone missing.

I put some music on, pull the blinds shut and lie down on the bed, so it's just me and my music. Nothing else matters.

I don't hear Dad's knock at the door. I must have fallen asleep.

He slowly walks towards my bed and sits down. He's got that *I-know-how-you-feel* look on his face.

'Mum said you've joined a club. That's great. If I'm honest, I didn't really get on with history at school. Couldn't see the point of it, if you see what I mean. Still, if it's your kind of stuff...' His voice trails off.

I don't say anything, but look up at his hopeful face.

'Do you still want to go to the game on Saturday? We could grab a burger and hot chocolate,' he says.

'Umm, I said I'd meet with Melanie and Ben on Saturday,' I say quietly.

Dad raises his eyebrows and pulls in his cheeks. 'Oh well, perhaps we can have a kick-about in the park on Sunday. Hey, why not invite that Melanie and Ben?'

I didn't see that one coming.

'Don't think Melanie plays football,' I say.

'What! You must be joking. I bet she's a demon with all those elbows flying about. No quarter given,' says Dad.

Dad looks tired. It must be all that travelling he does with his job, visiting different pharmacies. He doesn't look happy nowadays. He and Mum seem to be arguing a lot of the time.

He sighs. 'Anyway, where are you going? Cinema, bowling?'

'Not sure yet,' I mutter.

I can tell Dad is silently fuming. I know he wants to give me a good shake and kick-start me into action. He sort of holds his face in, so all the anger doesn't spill out.

'No problem, the important thing is you're going out with a couple of friends and that's real progress,' he says with mock cheer.

Progress. I hate that. Makes me sound like a project. A bit of clay, or playdough, that's moulded and shaped, to make something different.

I pick up my headphones and slump down onto the pillow, which is Dad's cue to leave. I don't feel like talking.

As Dad leaves, I ponder on the fact that I'm meant to be going back to Spinney Wood.

I feel my stomach churn as I think about Saturday and wonder if Melanie and Ben would get upset if I said I was ill. I probably will be ill anyway. It's inevitable the way I'm feeling now. I'll wake up Saturday morning and won't be able to get out of bed. I'll have a blinding headache, and the glare of the sun will make me dizzy.

But if I can get through Saturday, then I can look forward to doing nothing on Sunday. Just stay in bed and listen to my music. At least I made it into the woods today. That's more than I've done in months.

It will be Mum's turn to give me 'the talk' in a minute. She'll knock quietly on the door and come and sit down. She'll calmly talk about it being a *difficult time* for me, and she *knows what I'm going through*. Perhaps we can look at how I can plan Saturday, to make sure I don't get anxious!

No thanks.

I don't know why I can't tell them. But I can't. They wouldn't understand.

I think back to our trip to the woods today. Maybe Melanie isn't as annoying as I first thought. Irritating is probably nearer the mark. Still wanting to be in charge and super smooth, but she's not bad after you get to know her a bit, especially for a girl!

Perhaps I might just show up at Spinney Wood on Saturday after all.

TWELVE

Friday morning.

Melanie and Ben are waiting outside the school gates.

They're looking my way, and there's no way I can avoid them.

'League table out today,' chirps Ben. 'Great Goliath is aiming for the top spot.'

'In your dreams,' says Melanie with a half-smile. I can't help thinking she wants to say something else, but isn't sure how to.

We all walk slowly towards the staff car park. Even Ben is quiet, which is probably due to Melanie's orders.

Melanie suddenly stops and spins round to face me.

'Michael, when we were up at Spinney Wood, did you notice anything strange?'

She's fishing.

'Like what?'

Ben is about to interrupt, but a withering look from Melanie makes him think twice.

'Did anything odd strike you, like when Mr Logie appeared with his dog?' asks Melanie.

'He acted like he'd been zapped,' says Ben, pointing two fingers to resemble a gun. He blows imaginary smoke off his fingertips.

I moisten my lips. When they're bone dry I have to prise them open sometimes so I can speak.

'There was something...' I tentatively start. I've got their full attention now.

'What was it?' asks Melanie.

'I saw someone... someone else,' I try to explain.

'Who?' quizzes Melanie.

Ben has a completely blank face.

'I think...' I begin, 'I saw her eyes.'

My words are not coming out right. Not sure this is the right time.

'You can tell us, Michael. Your secret is safe with us, isn't it?' Melanie swerves round and eyeballs Ben.

'Yeah, scouts,' swears Ben, crossing himself.

'Her eyes... the woman's eyes... it was the same woman I saw Jonty with.' I suck in my cheeks and wait for the news to sink in.

Silence. I take a quick breath and continue.

'I saw her when Jonty followed me in the woods, that day after school.' I just say it.

Melanie nods for me to continue.

'It sort of just happened. One minute I was in Spinney Wood, the next I was in this sort of different world. It was warm and the sun was shining. I saw *her*.'

'So, this woman, you've actually met her?' asks Melanie.

'We didn't have an introduction as such,' I reply. 'But I saw her.'

'Like a time traveller!' says Ben, beaming.

'So who is she?' asks Melanie.

'Is she the *child catcher*?' says Ben excitedly.

Melanie and I choose to ignore Ben.

'So he's still in Spinney Wood – somewhere?' says Melanie, slowly and deliberately.

'Jonty?' cries Ben excitedly. He really is struggling to take in all this information.

'It's difficult to explain,' I tell Melanie.

'That's so cool,' says Ben. 'A real time traveller!' He smiles. Ben's mind has wandered off to a land far away.

'I've done some research about Spinney Wood, you know,' says Melanie confidently. 'There was a tribe that used to live there hundreds of years ago.'

'Yeah, I know. The Laco tribe,' I say. 'Mr Logie told me.'

'But they were massacred in a battle with another tribe. There were no survivors,' she adds.

Melanie looks puzzled.

We carry on walking along the pavement. The bell is about to ring, to signal five minutes until registration.

Melanie leans in towards me. I usually have to unscramble my brain when she does that.

'Mr Logie… he didn't want us to go any further in the wood yesterday,' she says.

'Yeah, it was like he saw something in the wood that scared him,' I reply.

'Jasper knew something was wrong. Dogs have this sixth sense, you know,' interjects Ben.

'Dogs always get spooked,' Melanie says curtly. 'They've got heightened senses and are highly intelligent… unlike some humans!' She positions her face in front of Ben.

'Just saying I think Jasper knows something as well,' says Ben defensively.

Melanie places her hands on her hips. 'How is *that* going to help us?'

'I sensed something in the woods, watching me,' I continue. 'I can't really explain it.' I shrug my shoulders.

Not sure where this is all going.

'Jasper smelt something,' continues Ben, undeterred. 'That's why he got spooked. Like a rotting body.'

'Really? And did *you* see any rotting bodies?' Melanie asks Ben pointedly.

'I've passed homeless people underneath shop windows, sleeping rough. That smell… a bit like that,' muses Ben.

'No, you haven't!' Melanie says, dismissing Ben with a wave of her hand.

'There was something else,' I say. 'I'm not sure if you heard anything, but there was this sound, a throbbing kind of noise that the ground was making.'

Ben stares at me and then at Melanie.

'The whole area seemed to be alive with loads of energy coming from it. Didn't you feel it?' I plead.

Melanie's nose twitches, as though she's making her mind up. Ben just looks positively gormless.

I can't blame them. Who would believe me?

The bell for registration rings.

Ben jumps two steps at a time up the steps leading to the main doors.

'We need to have a chat with Mr Logie at lunchtime,' Melanie suggests.

Ben crouches down and takes a big leap to jump the final three steps. He lands on his side and rolls over. He's covered in dirt and dust. Mr Jones walks by, shaking his head.

'I don't think he can help find Jonty. He said as much,' I say.

I lift my shoulders to take off my rucksack. We pass through the glass doors to the main hall. Students hurry past.

Ben's eyes light up. 'Yeah, perhaps old Logie's a time traveller as well?' He chuckles. 'He's probably got a magic Tardis in his back garden.' A big grin spreads across his face.

I can feel my stomach knotting, beginning to make me want to go to the toilet.

'We could tell him we smelt something odd in the wood, like a rotting body,' Ben continues.

'There was definitely an odd smell when we were there.' Melanie sniffs in the general direction of Ben before we all troop off to registration.

*

Drama.

At least we can stop talking about Spinney Wood, and the eyes and dogs, and the funny smell, can't we?

I hate drama, and Miss Pearson is always, well, so dramatic!

I'm working with Melanie, Ben, Simon Harrison and Abi Linton for the best part of the lesson, as we look at *Lord of the Flies.*

Miss Pearson wants us to perform it at the end of the year for the rest of the school. Good luck with that.

She's wearing a brightly coloured headscarf and a flowery top. She floats around like she's a magic butterfly.

She's put us in small groups to discuss the book.

'It's all about anarchy,' says Abi.

'Annie who?' says a puzzled Ben.

'It's when society breaks down. There's no order around you,' explains Melanie.

Harrison looks vacant, so he won't be contributing.

I keep my head down. It's then I become aware Miss Pearson is hovering over me.

'It might be about two opposite political styles,' Abi says. The group focus on her as she tries to elaborate. 'You know, like an authoritarian regime versus a liberal one.'

'Excellent,' says Miss Pearson.

'Or two different themes, like power against love,' Melanie adds.

I squirm a bit when I hear the word *love*, because it's a grown-up word, and we don't talk about those sorts of things in our house. Perhaps I'll feel it more as I get older.

The group goes quiet, and I assume we're all trying to work out what Melanie has said, but all heads have turned to me.

Miss Pearson lowers her head, as though she expects me to speak.

I hate group work. All that trying to work out what to say, and worrying if what I say is going to be all right. I can never work out how I'll feel. So sometimes I say nothing and wait until the time's up and I can leave. Best to keep your thoughts inside, where they're safe. That's what Mole does.

'Oi, penny for them?' Abi Linton is waving her hand in front of my face.

'What. Sorry. Oh, I dunno… perhaps it's about a thin line between two different worlds,' I say, suddenly inspired.

Not sure why I said that. I feel a surge of nervous energy shooting through my body. My palms are sweating, and my mouth is dry. I bite my lip, as I'm tempted to say a lot more, and rock forwards and backwards excitedly in my chair.

'That's interesting, Michael. What sort of worlds?' says Miss Pearson. She leans inwards.

I'm looking straight ahead.

'Go on, Michael,' encourages Miss Pearson.

Crikey.

My bottom is beginning to lose contact with the seat as I watch all the faces turn to me in a mixture of admiration and puzzlement, although Harrison is definitely in the latter camp. I can see eyes smiling at me, and heads nodding in approval.

Jack Flash is rising and I feel flushed.

'What if there was a special world and you had powers to slip between different worlds?' I bounce on my seat.

'Interesting…' muses Miss Pearson. 'Why would you need to go between these different worlds?' she asks, trying to flush more information from me.

She doesn't convince me she knows what I'm talking about. She looks clueless.

'Because that's where part of you belongs,' pipes up Melanie.

We exchange looks, and I notice a slight smile on her face.

Miss Pearson has her mouth open, trying to keep up.

'Bit like travelling in a Tardis,' says Ben smugly.

That kills the discussion. Ben has brought everyone down to earth.

Except for Harrison, whose mind is almost definitely floating somewhere in space.

I'd been rocking on the two back legs of my chair as I imagined this other world. I suddenly stop swaying, and the chair thuds back on the floor.

I purse my lips together and try to give the impression that it's someone else's turn.

The class ends and splits up for lunch. I'm happy to go and eat my lunch in the great hall, with Melanie and Ben.

'Eegh, peanut butter!' Ben screws his face up as he sees what's in my sandwich.

'I liked what you said in drama,' says Melanie, changing the subject.

'Not sure why I said that actually,' I admit. Nor why Melanie said what she did.

She smiles and I half look away. Still, I can't stop myself bouncing on my chair, and I have to squeeze my elbows in tight against my sides to stop.

'C'mon, we've got to see Mr Logie,' says Melanie.

Showdown.

*

Wizard's Troops are still in second place after the result of the latest history test. Mr Logie reels the names off with no dramatic effect today. He seems quite agitated. He just trundles though the lesson.

As everyone begins to file out of the classroom, I wait for Melanie and Ben to put their books away.

I feel nervous and take a deep breath. The three of us amble towards his desk.

He briefly glances up and then back to his papers again.

'Sorry about yesterday. Not sure what the dog was doing.' He gives a weak laugh. 'Hope you all got home all right.'

'Yes, thanks, no problems, sir,' I say.

He hesitates and looks like he's going to say something else, but he carries on arranging his notes.

'Sir, do you think Jonty has disappeared like all the other children in Spinney Wood?' I start.

Mr Logie's bushy eyebrows shoot up.

'What gives you that idea?' he retorts.

'But it's possible?' replies Melanie.

Ben shifts about uneasily on his feet.

'Did you notice anything strange when we saw you there, sir?' I ask.

Mr Logie spins round. 'Yes, I noticed three children in a wood looking for goodness knows what! Especially you, Dobson! Standing around as though you'd seen a ghost!'

'But, sir, you saw something as well, didn't you?' I plead.

I can hear him chuntering under his breath. He balls his hands into fists.

'This is ridiculous!' he booms. 'With everything that's going on, I think none of you should be wandering about Spinney Wood. You've heard all the reports. It's just not safe!' And with that, he storms out.

Melanie, Ben and I stand completely still. We're stunned. I've never seen him that angry, except in Spinney Wood.

'Wow, never seen old Logie throw his toys out of the pram like that!' says Ben, surprised.

'Why doesn't he want to do anything about finding Jonty?' asks Melanie.

'Perhaps he can't,' I reflect.

Ben waits a few seconds, before circling around Mr Logie's desk. He starts looking at stuff that's supposed to be private.

'Look, old Logie's pen.' He holds it up. It's an orange pen that has 'Made in Amsterdam' on it.

He spots Mr Logie's briefcase on the floor by the desk, shoots a glance at Melanie and then at the door. It's quiet in the corridor.

Ben lifts the briefcase onto the desk and takes a peek inside.

'What are you doing?' I exclaim. 'You can't do that!'

'You'll be in such trouble if he catches you,' Melanie says. Only she's not exactly stopping him.

Ben takes a peek inside.

This is such a bad move. There may be private things in there.

He draws out a small framed photograph of a woman and boy. Melanie cranes her neck to get a look at it, before Ben drops it back into the briefcase.

He then pulls out a newspaper cutting. The same cutting Mr Logie showed me.

'What's this?' he asks, placing the paper on the desk.

I nervously shoot a look at the door.

'It's a story about Mr Logie's friend, who went missing twenty-five years ago.'

Melanie and Ben both look my way.

'The one I *told* you about,' I say, slightly annoyed.

Ben peers at the picture.

Melanie twists the cutting around and starts to skim read the article. '*This* is Mr Logie's friend?' she asks.

She runs her finger slowly down the report.

'Pen and paper! Quickly.'

'What?' I ask, wondering what she's up to.

'He's got a beak, like old Logie!' says Ben, studying the picture.

I hand Melanie a page from my notepad and a pen. She writes down the name and address of the missing boy from the report.

'We shouldn't be doing this. Mr Logie will be really upset if he finds out,' I plead.

'He showed you the article. So it should be okay if we see it… we're friends after all,' Melanie replies.

'Quick, put it back now.' She slides the cutting back into the briefcase. The slip of paper goes into her jacket.

I let the thought run round my mind that Melanie said we're friends.

THIRTEEN

Saturday morning.

We've made a plan to meet to explore Spinney Wood. Perhaps we'll find out more about where Jonty is and whatever I saw last time we were there.

Ben is standing near the old youth club, on the other side of Spinney Wood.

He's got his full khaki-coloured combat gear on, complete with a floppy grey hat that hides most of his face. He looks like he's going for a walk in the Australian outback. A bulky rucksack, which is almost as big as him, sits on his shoulders, causing him to tilt to one side.

'Hi,' I say, with as much cheer as I can muster.

Ben just looks me up and down, as if he's telling me I've forgotten something.

'We could be gone for hours,' is all he says. He

heaves the rucksack another foot off his shoulders to emphasise the point.

'What have you got in there?' I ask.

'Provisions, water, food, extra clothing… You can't be too sure what we'll find in there.'

We are well away from the shopping precinct and curious passers-by, although Ben makes me nervous just looking at him. He's hopping about like a barrel of ready dynamite, desperate to get going before he explodes.

'I remembered some binoculars,' he says, a satisfied smile on his face. 'They're really powerful.'

Melanie appears round the corner. She crosses the pavement and walks past the last few houses, before this side of the wood starts.

A shoulder bag swings loosely by her side. I glance at her as she strides purposely over. She looks different without her school uniform.

I wonder if *I* look different on a Saturday.

'Eleven o'clock,' she says, checking her watch. 'Got your phones? We need your number, Michael, in case we get lost.'

It's more like a command than a request. I fiddle around for my phone, and give Melanie and Ben my number.

'We shouldn't get lost, it's only Spinney Wood,' I reason.

'I've got a torch,' says Ben.

I shake my head.

'Good,' Melanie replies.

We'll only be a couple of hours at most, I reckon.

Hopefully.

We need to get going, as more people are milling around the precinct, and I can see that man who walks his dog. I move behind Ben's rucksack, so he doesn't spot me.

Ben's bag is seriously packed. It towers above his head, pushing his whole body forward.

'You okay with all this, Michael?' Melanie tilts her head to one side in that patronising way she has.

'We need to be careful, that's all I'm saying,' I reply, trying to convince myself it's only a walk in the woods.

At least I'm outside and not listening to Mum droning on about not doing *normal* stuff. She won't know where I am anyway. Uncle Steven won't say anything.

A partially enclosed pathway leads us away from the housing estate and into the woods.

Despite the time of day, as soon as we hit the woods, we lose a lot of the natural light. Silence surrounds us. Even the distant rumbling of cars in the distance quickly fades. At first, the path is well trodden and easy to follow, but soon the dense undergrowth and thick bushes make it less easy to negotiate.

Melanie puts her hand up and we halt.

'We were over there on Friday, which is the way to the canal. We need to follow this way.'

'No, definitely this way,' I say confidently, pointing in a different direction, and brush past Melanie.

'O... *kay*,' she says, stretching the word out to show her surprise.

'We need to look out for a circle of ancient stones which is about half a mile over there, where you can see the fields,' she says.

'Ancient stones?' I ask.

'I've looked it up and it says there used to be an ancient tribe that worshipped there. They used the stones as some sort of meeting place,' she explains.

'That makes sense. They've found things that belonged to the Laco tribe there. Stuff they used every day,' I add.

Ben looks at me in a way which suggests I've earned me some points. Even Melanie seems quite impressed.

'Bet they had red and blue paint all over their bodies, and stripped naked when they went into battle. The ancient Britons did that,' says Ben.

He's off again.

Melanie ignores him.

'They'd scream at the top of their voices when they charged, and they had these wooden spears above their heads to scare the enemy,' Ben continues. There's no stopping him when he gets like this.

He charges round a small clump of dead tree trunks, squawking at the top of his voice.

'Did he say anything else, Mr Logie, I mean?' says Melanie, shaking her head despairingly at Ben.

'No,' I say.

'Anything about a *child catcher*?' Ben sings out. He's slipping off the radar again.

I picture Mr Logie in the back of my mind. His beak is pecking at my shoulder and his beady eyes are staring through me.

Now that Ben has calmed down, we resume our walk. The crisp, chilly air is quite pleasant. The only sounds are birdsong high above and the rustle of clothing brushing against undergrowth as we march into the heart of the wood.

After twenty minutes, we approach a clearing. There are a couple of dead tree trunks on their sides. We stop and sit down to have a drink and a snack.

Ben hauls his rucksack off his back, and takes a flask of hot chocolate out. He hands out a couple of small cups.

I start to feel guilty that I hadn't thought of bringing anything to eat or drink, and think perhaps Ben isn't so daft after all.

We sit on the tree trunk, legs dangling over the side, and I suddenly feel glad I didn't go to the football with Dad.

I've even forgotten about the face and eyes I saw the other day. Well, just for a moment anyway.

I can't imagine why Jonty hasn't gone back home. For starters, it would have saved us all the bother of being in Spinney Wood. I say as much out loud.

Melanie gives this some thought. 'My mum said his mum is always out or leaving him on his own,' she says.

Ben's eyes suddenly light up. 'Aliens have probably taken him! A mega-beam has circled Jonty and put him in a trance. Some steps have come down from their spacecraft, and he's been taken hostage to another planet!'

No, I was right about Ben.

Melanie continues her line of thought. 'I saw his mum yesterday in the shops. She didn't seem bothered. Just chatting as normal, as though she didn't care much he'd gone missing,' she says.

'Or been *murdered*…' whispers Ben.

'The police haven't said he's been murdered,' I say, tutting.

'They can't. It's still a missing person enquiry until they find worms eating the insides of his stomach,' Ben says confidently.

'Ben!' Melanie glares at him, and he lowers his head and carries on drinking his chocolate.

'Just saying,' he mumbles.

We finish our drinks and move on. The sandy path has now disappeared, and thistles and dock are strewn across our way. I attempt to negotiate the clearest path.

Dark, ominous clouds scurry across the sky and the first drops of rain begin to fall. They start to hit the crisp, crackly leaves beneath our feet, and soon the rain gathers pace.

I turn the collar of my jacket up as I try and work out which way to go.

'What is it?' asks Melanie.

Huge trees tower over us, blocking our path. It's not obvious which way to go.

'Dead end,' announces Ben.

'You're lost, aren't you, Michael?' accuses Melanie.

I can't understand. It was so easy before… I knew what to do. But the mass of branches and brambles are shutting us out. The trees are pushing us away, like sentries guarding a treasure.

'We're here!' bellows Ben at the top of his voice.

The trees are motionless. It's completely silent.

'This is a complete waste of time.' Melanie glares at me.

I was sure I would find the eyes.

'There's definitely no way through here. I thought you knew where you were going, Michael?' Melanie sounds disappointed.

'Yeah, perhaps the *child catcher* has Saturdays off,' says Ben sarcastically.

The rain is driving hard in our faces. The beech trees seem to huddle even closer, barring our path.

Perhaps Mr Logie was right after all.

We should have stayed away.

I've given it my best shot, and we've found nothing.

FOURTEEN

'Oh, Michael, you're back! I thought you'd be out longer. Is everything all right with your friends?'

'Yeah, we just went for a walk.'

I spy Uncle Steven reading the newspaper by the fire. Mum fixes her eyes on my shoes.

'Look at your muddy shoes! Where have you been? Leave them by the door. I've spent the whole morning cleaning the house, and look what you've done. For goodness' sake, you wear those for school. Where have you been to get them so dirty?'

Uncle Steven throws me a quizzical glance, before returning to his newspaper.

I mumble something about being sorry, and turn around so she can't get another good look at the black leather layered in mud.

She suddenly mellows. 'Still, if you've been

somewhere nice, I don't suppose it really matters.'

I slip off my shoes and leave them on the mat by the door.

My corduroy coat is soaked, and I hang it behind the front door, flinging my jumper over the warm radiator.

Mum grabs my jumper and grubby jeans, and scurries upstairs with more dirty washing.

'So, what has Sherlock discovered today?' Uncle Steven says quietly.

'Oh, nothing much,' I say, unable to hide my disappointment. 'But I think our history teacher knows about Jonty.'

'Here, I did a bit of digging around.' Uncle Steven opens his laptop and scrolls down to show me various links about missing children and Spinney Wood.

'It appears there's a connection between Spinney Wood, an ancient burial site and missing children,' he says, tapping his nose.

'I know,' I reply, keeping my voice low. I glance upstairs and move closer to Uncle Steven.

'But we found nothing.'

Suddenly Uncle Steven's arm springs backwards and flies into my face.

'Ouch!' I say, grimacing.

'Sorry, you okay? Afraid it's happening more often lately,' he says glumly.

'Yeah, fine,' I say, feeling my mouth. 'You all right?'

'Can't complain,' he says with a deadpan face, then grins.

'No good complaining anyway.' I carry the joke through.

I can hear Mum coming back down the stairs.

'Keep us up to speed, maestro, eh?' Uncle Steven winks.

'Will do!' I shoot past Mum and dash upstairs to the bathroom.

Time for a warm bath. I fish out a fresh pair of pants, a clean top, and jeans from the bedroom drawer.

A bath is safe.

The sound of running water drowns out any voices, and I've taken everything off that I wore in the woods. I can start again and things will be the same. Back to normal. Tea will be at five o'clock.

Dad will be home by then, and he'll chat about the game. I expect City will win.

I relax in the warm soapy suds and shut my eyes, drifting off listening to my music. I can be anywhere in my head. I don't have to worry about doing drama on Monday, or playing silly games like 'Kerplunk'.

It's nice and cosy. The bubbles block everything out. I can carry on like this. Nothing has changed. Mole will be fine.

Spaghetti bolognese for tea. I'm starving. Although at the weekends I'm usually hungrier, especially as the day seems to drag a bit.

When I come back downstairs, Uncle Steven is asleep with the newspaper on his lap.

Mum is getting the table ready and scurrying

between the kitchen and the lounge. She's chatting away as she puts a hot dish in the centre of the table.

'So, Michael, where did you go with your friends?'

'Oh, just a walk,' I say. I've been caught unawares. I should have planned what I was going to say.

'I know that. But where?' Mum swings her head from side to side in a jokey way, although I know she isn't joking.

'Melanie and Ben wanted me to go,' I say, hoping that will suffice as an answer.

'Where did you go? Simple question!' Mum's chuntering beneath her breath.

'Spinney Wood,' I mumble, and wait for it.

She flings her fork down hard on her plate, metal on metal. The clanging makes me jump back in my chair.

'Spinney Wood!' she shouts, her eyes ablaze. 'What did I tell you about not going there?'

Uncle Steven wakes suddenly.

I stare at the polished table and yearn for my music, to drown out her screeching voice.

'You could have fallen over and been hurt, got lost, or, worse still, you could have gone missing.' And she shakes her head in a way that makes me want to burrow even further underground.

'Cut him some slack, Debs,' Uncle Steven pleads.

'I've warned him before about going there,' Mum says.

Everything happens around me, as if I'm not here. Mum's words swirl around my head before crashing down on my numb brain as I wait for the storm to pass over. It's just noise now. The force of her anger rises and then falls as quickly, as I sense a lull.

'Did Melanie's and Ben's mothers know you were up at Spinney Wood?' she asks.

'Don't know,' I reply. Which is true.

'What can happen when they're out together? They've got a good vibe going. Leave them,' Uncle Steven says.

Mum ignores Uncle Steven.

'Spinney Wood isn't safe. How many times do I need to tell you!'

'We've seen Mr Logie up there before,' I splutter.

'*What!*'

'Mr Logie walks his dog in Spinney Wood.'

'I expect he's been encouraging you to explore that wood. He doesn't seem to realise it's not a safe place for a twelve-year-old to be.'

'No, he hasn't.' I lift my head and meet Mum's eyes. 'We just happened to meet him there one day.'

'There you go,' says Uncle Steven. 'Even one of his teachers goes up there,' he concludes.

Mum's face twitches, and I can feel her anger simmering, but it's true. It's all true.

Mum turns on Uncle Steven. 'What would you know about being safe?'

He bites his lip and hides behind his newspaper.

Suddenly I'm not that hungry anymore and push my plate away.

'What are you doing? You haven't finished your spaghetti bolognese,' Mum shouts.

'I don't want it.'

'I'm only thinking of you, Michael. You've heard the news this week about that wood, haven't you? It's not safe.'

A drum is banging in my head, and it won't stop. It just goes on and on, getting louder.

I draw breath and stop. For a second, I wonder where I am. A muzzy fog descends. I can't think.

Suddenly I bolt upright and I'm back in the lounge with the spaghetti bolognese.

'I don't need to tell you everything!' I shoot the words out.

I watch Mum's eyes widen and blaze with fury and she yells, 'I'm your mother, remember!'

I dash upstairs, and my legs almost buckle beneath me.

Slamming my door, I put my headphones on and try to calm myself, but my breathing is loud, and my heart is thumping painfully.

I bury my head in the duvet, gripping it and stuffing it in my mouth, and gently rock to and fro with the music.

My muscles are tense, and I squeeze my body to try and fit myself into the space. Slowly, I let go of the duvet, but keep my head under it, where it's warm and safe.

Mole should never have gone out today. He should have stayed at home. None of this would have happened.

I finally start to relax, and wonder whether I should go back downstairs. Mole knows what I feel. He understands and he's always there. I can always come to Mole.

The front door closes. Dad is back from the football.

Dad and Mum will be talking about me. I turn the music up louder to drown out their voices.

How could I go missing? I was with Melanie and Ben. And anyway, it's only an ordinary wood. It's not like it's the Amazon forest, or anything.

My mind turns to Melanie. There's no doubt she can be irritating. And she has this annoying habit of just taking control and being in charge of things.

But I don't mind.

Mum's different. She wants to know *everything*. She's always telling me what I can and can't do. What I should do and where I should go… all to make sure her world is fine.

But she doesn't need to know everything.

I know what to do.

FIFTEEN

I like Sundays, as I can have a really long lie-in.

Except today I wake early and can't get back to sleep.

My bleary eyes are half-closed. It's dead quiet.

I pull the duvet up around my head, then peek out of the corner of it and glance at the clock on the bedside drawer.

Nana will be here soon and it'll be all right for a bit. Then they'll start to argue.

It's always over something trivial. But it goes on and on, until she leaves. We won't see her again for ages.

I roll slowly out of bed and stand in front of the mirror. The mop on top of my head is always worse first thing in the morning. But it's not first thing. More like eleven o'clock.

I stifle a yawn, pull on my jeans and yank an old T-shirt over my head.

Running a brush through my hair takes longer. I guess I do need my hair cut.

I check my phone and there's a message from Melanie. *Bit of a waste of time yesterday, but still enjoyed the day.*

I suppose I did as well, but wish we could have found *something* in Spinney Wood. Or *someone.*

I'll see her tomorrow at school. Not going to reply now.

The doorbell goes. It's Nana.

'Can you get that?' Mum calls to Dad from the kitchen. 'I'm busy.'

'So I'm not busy then!' Dad shouts back angrily.

After a few seconds, I hear Dad slam something down on the floor, before moving into the hallway.

The door is opened and I can hear him asking Nana into the house.

I slide open my bedroom door and wait quietly on the landing. Just to gauge the atmosphere.

I meander down the stairs. Nana sees me out of the corner of her eye.

'Goodness me, you do need a haircut, Michael,' she gasps, staring at my mop.

'Yeah, I know,' I agree, waving a hand airily over the curls.

I come round the armchair and kiss her lightly on the cheek.

'Let's have a look at you then,' she says, thrusting a hand out, indicating for me to move a few paces from her. 'How is your new school?' she asks, fixing me with a stare.

'Not bad,' I say, and nod.

'Made any friends?'

'Friends?' Dad says with a smirk.

'Yes, a couple,' I reply, still standing to attention.

Dad rolls his eyes.

Not sure what it is about Nana, but she's always a bit frosty when she comes to see us.

Uncle Steven appears down the hallway and smiles in the direction of his mother. He manoeuvres over to where she is sitting.

Nana immediately gets up, and a big smile washes over her face. It's as though someone's changed her channel.

'Hello, darling, how are you?' she gushes.

'Oh, not bad,' he says, looking up at Dad, who turns away.

Mum stands in the doorway and takes off her oven gloves. 'Hello, Mum, you found us all right then?'

'Bit off the beaten track, aren't you? Would you believe it, there was also some youngsters zigzagging down the road in front of my car. Throwing drink cartons on the ground as if they couldn't care less!' Nana blazes.

No one knows how to respond to this.

'Dinner will be about half past twelve,' says Mum, turning around abruptly before disappearing into the kitchen.

Nana gazes at her lap.

It's clear she doesn't like the area, but at least we're near my school.

'Deborah moved to be nearer me, Mum. You knew that,' points out Uncle Steven.

Dad gives a deep sigh.

'Well, it's not bad, I suppose. Bit on the small side,' Nana says, glancing around the lounge.

'I'll be able to see Kevin and Deborah more often. It makes perfect sense,' points out Uncle Steven.

'You need to keep an eye on your health,' Nana warns him. 'How is your job going? Everything okay?'

'Meetings, deadlines, usual things,' Uncle Steven says.

Nana looks at him, her expression serious. 'Be careful. You don't want to get ill, do you?'

Uncle Steven grabs her hand and squeezes it. 'I will. I'll be careful. Promise.'

'So there's enough space for you to have your own room here?' Nana peers over to his bedroom, off the hall.

'Three bedrooms,' snaps Dad.

'It's just with one wage earner, there's sometimes not enough room for guests,' Nana says.

'Guests?' Mum comes storming out of the kitchen. 'Do you think that's what Steven is? A guest!'

Dad shakes his head before marching off in the direction of the garage, no doubt looking for a bit of peace.

Mum glares at Nana, before turning back to the kitchen.

'Now what have I said?' asks Nana defensively.

I'm not sure whether I should creep back to my room and leave Nana talking to Uncle Steven.

'Now tell me all about this new job you have,' Nana gushes to him. 'I hear you were on their wanted list!'

'Well, not exactly, but it's a good fit,' Uncle Steven admits.

Nana leans over to where he's sitting. 'Well, at least one of you has the brains to get on,' she chuckles.

Nana smiles at me as though I should get her joke.

I twitch nervously and Uncle Steven bites his lip.

At least she'll be gone after lunch.

SIXTEEN

Monday lunchtime.

We walk slowly along the corridor towards the cloakrooms. We've finished morning lessons. Time for lunch.

'So what happens next?' asks Ben.

Melanie gives me a cold, long stare.

'What?' I say defensively.

'We're not exactly making much progress, are we?' says Melanie, slipping her books into her locker.

She sounds disappointed. I don't blame her.

Not sure what happened on Saturday. I thought I had it figured out. Knew how to find the eyes.

Funny thing is, it seems normal at school without Jonty now. It's quieter for starters. There's also more room to walk in the corridors.

'What do you mean?' I say.

'We only have your word, Michael,' Melanie says fiercely. 'I mean, how can we be sure it was ever true?' She turns, facing me head-on.

I gulp and step back. 'I'm not making it up, if that's what you think! Why would I do that?' I ask, astonished.

She bites her bottom lip and folds her arms as she strolls down the corridor.

'Even if Jasper is a bit of a thicko, what about Mr Logie's dog?' asks Ben, as we catch up with her.

I sense a slither of hope.

'That's right. Two dogs can't be wrong,' I say.

Melanie scrunches up her nose.

'Pity we couldn't ask the dogs what they saw. That would cut to the chase,' says Ben with a grin.

Melanie looks tempted to give him one of her withering looks, but then simply says, 'C'mon, let's have lunch.'

We find a table near the back of the hall and get our lunch boxes out.

The full-length windows, either side of the great hall, let in the sun's weak rays.

Ben's freckles seem brighter in the light.

I start to count them when Melanie suddenly interrupts my thoughts.

She puts her salad box down on the table and announces, 'So what do we know?'

Ben stares blankly at her for a second, before he realises she's talking about Spinney Wood.

'Oh right, well, there's the child catcher, kids go

missing over the years, and you and old Logie are Time Lords,' he says, and thrusts his head towards me.

Ben has summed it up.

'The same bad thing that happened years ago is happening today, and in the same place,' I say, with as much urgency as I can muster.

But that doesn't get us any nearer to finding Jonty.

My mouth dries up, and my windpipe feels as though it's filled with lots of jumbled words. It's like cling film stretched over my mouth, preventing me from saying anything else.

'Was there anything else, Michael? *Anything* you can remember?' implores Melanie.

'Not really... I didn't want to look. Except,' I start, 'there were other voices, in the distance. But I didn't see anything specific.'

'Others?' says Melanie.

'Who?' says Ben.

'Don't know. But they must have been close to where this woman and Jonty were,' I reply with confidence.

'Interesting...' Melanie mulls it over.

I look at Melanie and her eyes light up.

'Bit of a coincidence, don't you think?' she says. 'Other children go missing. Now Jonty?'

'Like hostage-taking!' exclaims Ben, a bit too loudly for my liking.

I glance around to see if anyone is looking at us, as Ben jerks his head sideways frenetically.

'You do believe me, don't you?' I say desperately.

'I want to believe you, Michael.' She turns to Ben. 'We both do, don't we?'

'Suppose,' says Ben, nonplussed.

'It must be that old woman that's been taking children,' I say.

'The one we can't see. The one *you* can't see!' Melanie says sarcastically.

'The *curse* of Spinney Wood!' Ben pulls a face like a gargoyle, revealing a toothy grin. He curls his hands over his mouth, takes a big breath and blows a noise like a trumpet… an out-of-tune trumpet.

Heads turn in the canteen to see where the strange sound is coming from.

Lots of little wrinkles appear on Melanie's forehead, and she shakes her head at Ben.

I don't care where Jonty is, as long as it's not here in school. His name still sends a shiver down my spine.

We don't have to find Jonty, do we? A carousel of disturbing thoughts swings round and round my brain. I cling on and wait for them to stop. I feel sick and sweaty, and my chest is heaving. It's getting out of control. All I can hear is the whirring of branches, of angry trees.

I slowly put down my peanut butter sandwich, and lower my head.

'So we know where Jonty is – he's in the woods somewhere – but we can't find him!'

Ben pulls a goofy face and scratches his head. 'Logic, boys and girls, is your guide,' he says, doing an uncanny impersonation of Mr Yates.

Silence.

'Well, we couldn't find him on Saturday,' Melanie says, shrugging her shoulders.

'We need a plan to rescue him!' Ben's brain has suddenly called up a commando unit, and is ready to mount a daring plan.

'No, we can't,' I say calmly. 'I mean, I don't like Jonty, and I don't think he liked me,' I start, and they both stare at me in disbelief.

'*Like?* He wanted to alter your face, remember?' Melanie reminds me.

'I don't want to see Jonty again – I know what he'd like to do to me, when he sees me. But he was in the woods with that woman. I saw him with her. She has these eyes which draw you to her. It's like an energy pulling you. It's her – that woman – drawing you towards this... this other world.' I'm struggling to find the right words. Everything I say sounds weird.

'Two different worlds then?' smiles Melanie. 'Like a portal where you can travel between worlds.' She turns to me, smiling.

Kind of makes sense.

'Where Michael and old Logie can travel between worlds,' Ben corrects Melanie.

'And space,' Melanie adds.

'And if Mr Logie won't do anything, then it's down to our very own Time Lord.' Ben slaps my back, which makes me shudder.

'Wish we could all go there together... to this other

world,' says Melanie.

I feel all warm inside. I don't feel alone, even if I am.

A larger-than-life picture of Jonty flexing his muscles suddenly floods my mind.

What if Jonty is really happy? I mean, perhaps he doesn't want to be found. Perhaps he's glad to have disappeared forever?

SEVENTEEN

Evening meal has finished.

Dad and Uncle Steven are talking football in the lounge.

Mum has finished the washing-up and put the plates and cutlery away. She then goes through the same routine: closes the garden gate; locks back and front doors; make sure all the windows are closed; shoes are all cleaned for the next day.

She seems to be edgy tonight.

'I've got a meeting to prepare for tomorrow,' announces Dad. He rises from his chair. He strides off to the back room, which doubles up as a study.

Mum glares at him as he leaves.

She joins me on the sofa and shuffles close to me. She seems to be searching for the right words.

'Michael, your dad and I have an appointment

tomorrow. Uncle Steven will be here when you get home from school,' she says.

She's not telling me everything.

'What sort of appointment?' I ask.

Mum fidgets around and rubs her fingers down her trouser legs.

'Dad and I are having a few problems at the moment... and we just need a bit of help to sort ourselves out. Nothing for you to worry about, though,' she says, running her hand through my hair.

If I was normal, had loads of friends and did normal things, I'm sure they wouldn't need an 'appointment.'

I know why they have to see someone. They snap and shout at each other all the time; they're clearly not getting on very well.

I know Mum is worried about me. More than usual now.

I feel trapped. I want to make things right.

I should say something. But I can't, so Mum feels the need to fill the silence.

'It'll be all right,' she tries to reassure me. 'It's just a bit difficult at the minute, so we thought we needed to talk to someone.'

'Who?' I ask.

'A marriage counsellor,' Mum says quietly.

Uncle Steven remains tight-lipped.

Mum gets up slowly and heads upstairs. Her footsteps sound heavy on the stairs and landing. I hear her walk into her bedroom and quietly close the door.

Uncle Steven wheels over to where I'm sitting. He squeezes my hand. 'It'll be all right, Michael,' he reassures me. 'Lots of couples have problems from time to time.'

Will it be all right? Uncle Steven can't know that for sure. Nobody can know that.

'So, how are Melanie and Ben?' He changes the subject.

I stop mulling over Mum's announcement and sit up straighter to clear my head. 'They're fine,' I say. 'You remember Mr Logie, the history teacher? He knows where Jonty is as well!'

'Inspector Dobson, that's amazing. But if he knows where the boy is, then why hasn't this Mr Logie gone to the police?' Uncle Steven looks puzzled.

'Not sure. He's none too pleased with me at the moment. He thinks I'm just a kid who's too nosy for his own good.' I shrug my shoulders.

'You, my man, are totally believable. You need to follow your hunch.'

Uncle Steven makes it sound so simple.

He goes to open his mouth. He's struggling with his face, and his mouth twists uncontrollably for a few seconds. He gulps hard and then smiles.

'I'm seeing the specialist on Friday. Probably change my meds,' he says.

'Listen, why don't you speak to one of your teachers, someone who will listen,' he points out. 'If your budget doesn't stretch to additional support, here's a little help.' He presses a pound coin into my hand.

'You needn't do that,' I say, slowly shoving it into my pocket.

Mum has come downstairs and is back in the lounge.

Hope she didn't hear anything.

'Drink, anyone?' she asks.

'Cup of tea would be good,' says Uncle Steven.

Mum's gaze lingers on me, and I shoot her a puzzled glance.

Something else is eating at her.

'Uncle Steven will be going back to his house on Thursday. Thought you'd like to know, Michael, in case you're planning anything.' She gives a little smile.

'Oh,' I say, surprised.

'Like walking across the top of the O2?' jokes Uncle Steven.

She forces a smile. 'I wouldn't put it past you, that's all.' She shrugs her shoulders and lets out a sigh.

'Sorry, mate. I was going to tell you but it went out of my mind, that's all,' he says.

I nod my head, wanting to understand.

'Anyway, Michael shouldn't be out in this cold weather. He catches a chill easily.'

'No, I don't,' I challenge Mum. 'I'm hardly allowed out!'

'I know what Uncle Steven is like. He'd have you out on midnight walks, if it was down to him,' Mum replies sharply.

'Well, it wouldn't be… he can't do this and can't do that,' I say.

An awkward silence descends.

'You never did tell me how you had your accident, Uncle Steven,' I say, changing the subject.

'Trying to rescue some damsel in distress stuck up a tree,' he says light-heartedly. His face hangs downwards.

But no one laughs.

EIGHTEEN

Uncle Steven's words are still ringing in my ears as I climb the stairs at the end of the corridor. Mr Yates' maths classroom is the last room on the left.

I'll tell him what I know.

Mr Yates has this funny habit of stroking his pointed beard, which some of the boys mimic.

As I hover outside the room, I can see he's sitting down sipping a cup of tea.

He's always very smart and wears thick-rimmed glasses. He often peers over them when he talks to you. He also walks in a regimented fashion as though he's on parade. His shoes must have metal studded heels, as you hear him coming a mile off.

He looks up when I knock.

I grit my teeth and have no idea how he's going to respond to what I'm about to say.

I try and assure myself teachers won't take sides.

'Enter!' he announces in a sergeant major voice. I mean he's loud and clear.

He eyes me as I slowly enter his classroom.

'Come in, Dobson,' he says, ushering me in.

'Sir,' I nervously begin as I fiddle with my fingers. 'It's about Jonathan Johnson, sir.'

Mr Yates aligns the books he has completed marking in a tidy pile. He pushes the unmarked books to one side.

He signals for me to continue.

'Well, it's just that I know where he is,' I say.

He looks unfazed. 'Go on.'

'The thing is, sir, I think Mr Logie does as well.'

Mr Yates gets up, strokes his beard and walks over to the window. He glances back at the door to make sure it's shut.

I can feel my heart beating faster. It's now or never…

'He knows all about Spinney Wood, sir,' I burst out.

'What is the connection between Spinney Wood and Mr Logie?' he asks.

I have lots of jumbled thoughts bouncing around like spring coils. I can't control them.

'Well, I think Mr Logie knows something about this woman from a tribe that lived a long time ago. She lives in Spinney Wood… but not really… if you see what I mean. She's the one who keeps taking children.' I lower my head, afraid to see the look on his face.

'I'm afraid I don't see what you mean,' Mr Yates says calmly.

Mr Yates is always talking about using your logic to work out things. *Reason, boys and girls, is your great friend*, he often reminds us.

Ben's freckled face pops into my mind.

Mr Yates stands with his arms behind his back, gazing out of the window.

My head is swirling with fogginess, squeezing any logic completely out of my brain!

It's all gone quiet.

I glance up and watch Mr Yates tickling his beard.

I'm not sure if I should leave. Coming here hasn't really helped.

He swivels round and stares at me. 'How on earth do you know this? Where is your proof, Dobson?' he says.

I feel my shoulders drop. Mole is searching for a nice, quiet spot underground.

'Yes,' he says with a deep sigh. 'I see it's a bit of an ordeal for you, Dobson. I'll give it some thought. Off you go.'

I turn and slope out of the classroom.

At the top of the stairs, I lean against the wall and look down on the students jostling each other below.

It feels like I'm trapped in a giant bubble, floating around. Everything suddenly slows down. I'm on the outside, looking in on my world.

Abi Linton is turning her hand up and down to show off her nails to Sue Nicholls, waving them in the air like a princess. They giggle, and big smiles light up their faces as they breeze down the corridor, oblivious to me.

Harrison and Pierce meander down the corridor, shirts hanging out of their trousers and their hair ruffled. They're probably heading in the wrong direction for class. They don't see me either.

Ben is marching down the corridor. His little legs cover the ground at a rate of knots as though he's on manoeuvres, but without his rucksack. He's looking straight ahead. His mouth is shut tight as he bobs up and down, probably picturing himself charging up a hill to take an enemy stronghold.

The corridor quietens down and my back is cold against the long mural on the wall. I turn to study it more closely. I've never really noticed it before. I pull away slightly, to get a better look. There's a bow of a ship that was once famous. It was made in our town, and it went to war somewhere. But peering closer, I can see the black paint of the once-famous battleship is peeling and starting to fade.

It needs a lick of paint. The sails are patchy and the guns have lost their colour. They're only little things, but I can see them.

I should disappear to the library, or the common room. Hide and be safe. But Mole just wants to stay here. I don't have to pretend I'm interested in what's being said. I don't have to make an effort to join in things.

The hall floor needs cleaning. The tiles are all muddied from this morning's stampede. I reckon every other square tile needs scrubbing.

I jump as a face suddenly appears under my chin. Bright blue eyes stare at me like a goldfish.

'Wakey, wakey, lessons started five minutes ago,' says Melanie.

Her words are mumbled and her mouth is swollen; it's like she's got several marbles in one cheek.

'Oh, I didn't realise that was the time,' I reply. I straighten my back, turning my wrist over to check my watch. 'What are you doing here anyway?'

'Dentist. Mum couldn't get an after-school appointment, so Mr Jones said it was okay to go during school hours on this occasion.'

She studies my face carefully. 'I have to say, Michael, you don't look well.'

'I'm fine,' I lie, without meeting her gaze.

'No, I can definitely tell. You look like you've seen a ghost.' She lowers her head, to try and get me to focus on her.

I've seen her do this before. Like a praying mantis. She'll just stay here until she gets an answer.

She folds her arms and takes a deep breath. 'Look, I know you think I'm slightly odd, all matter-of-fact and pretending I know all the answers.'

I shoot her a glance. Her eyes start to sparkle, and I find myself breaking into a smile.

'I thought Melony Magic knew everything?' I say.

'So what if I love history and…' she pauses, '…the league table show I'm not bad, in fact.' She raises her nose in the air, tossing her head upwards for full effect.

'Yeah, right.' I smile.

'I've told Mr Yates everything.' I bite my lip.

'What did he say?'

'Not much.' I turn my head away and start studying the mural again. 'So nothing we can do now, eh?'

'*We* can't do anything,' she stresses, 'but *you* can.' And a gleam catches her eyes.

NINETEEN

No test or league table in history today.

Mr Logie is off sick. He looked really pale and puffy yesterday. I hope I haven't made him ill.

It's break time. We're hanging around on the playing fields before heading to the science lab.

'I reckon Spinney Wood is hiding a terrible secret,' Melanie says thoughtfully.

'And now Mr Logie isn't even here to help,' I reply.

'Yeah, we've no idea when he'll be back at school either,' she says.

Ben's face lights up, the way it does when one of his ideas launches with full force into his head. 'We've still got that address from the newspaper,' he says excitedly. He pushes his freckled face into mine.

I lean back, slightly uneasy about even having the address.

'Perhaps this friend's mother knows Mr Logie,' suggests Melanie.

'But she won't know about the eyes,' I say glumly. 'The eyes hold the key. I'm sure of it. The eyes and this mystery woman are the gateway into this other world,' I say.

'Eyes!' shouts Ben. 'That's what spooked Jasper. He sees things in the dark we can't see.'

'You said he has cataracts,' retorts Melanie. 'He's blind as a bat.'

'Not in the dark, he isn't,' Ben says, momentarily offended.

We find an unoccupied bench and sit down.

'Anyway, it seems that Mr Logie and Michael are the only ones who can see the eyes,' Melanie says. She ponders this for a moment then turns to me. 'What's so special about the eyes, Michael?'

'They kind of hold you... like they want you.' I swallow hard.

'Bit like a memory card planted in your brain, so you're programmed to behave in a certain way,' theorises Ben. 'Like a Cyberman ordered to destroy the world by a computer.'

Ben's been watching too many Marvel movies.

'Not sure what Mr Yates made of what I said,' I say.

'That's all right,' Ben reassures me. 'He'll take ages to process all that stuff.'

Ben rocks from side to side with his fingers on the side of his head, pretending to join up wires.

'Why do you always have to be so dramatic?' asks Melanie with a sigh.

Immediately, all sorts of questions surface in my mind. Should I tell Mum about all this now? She'd have kittens if she knew, but then again, she's always banging on about doing stuff and not staying in your room.

Suddenly school doesn't seem to matter anymore. Lessons and tests aren't important. A surge of warmth runs through my body. I kind of feel weirdly connected to Melanie and Ben.

Mole isn't alone.

But I don't want to dress up as Jack Flash and pretend that I'm in control. To keep the mask on until the show has finished.

'Wish *I* could see the eyes,' Ben says, and frowns. He rolls his eyes and moves his head in a kind of circle. Slowly at first, then speeds up.

Melanie shakes her head and Ben lurches backwards, falling off the bench and onto the grass.

We all laugh.

'I think the wood chooses you,' I say. 'The trees controls who gets to see the old woman.'

'Makes sense,' Melanie nods.

'Oh, chosen one!' Ben holds his hands aloft, bowing down exaggeratedly.

It's difficult not to smile.

'When I was checking the library archives it said they found human bones scattered in Spinney Wood,' pipes up Melanie.

'It was the scene of a massacre, wasn't it?' I reply.

'Well, remember what you said about all that energy in Spinney Wood? Maybe it's leftover negative energy that's come from the massacre,' Melanie explains.

She could be right, I think.

'So what?' asks Ben, confused.

'Well, energy can sometimes transport people or things, from one place to another,' I follow up.

'Oh, I get it!' says Ben, pleased with himself. 'Like a space traveller going through time.'

'Bit like your brain trying to catch up then,' Melanie says, and shoves Ben back off the bench.

We're going to be late for science, so we start to troop back to the labs.

Melanie's quiet for once. Then she suddenly stops in her tracks, her eyes wide. 'So that's why she's been able to take children over the years! And that's where Mr Logie's friend must be,' she concludes.

'So Mr Logie *knows* where his friend is!' exclaims Ben.

'We don't know for sure,' I say. 'Anyway, we need to concentrate on finding Jonty. That's what this is all about,' I say purposely.

'What if old Logie and his friend are in it together?' Ben suggests.

'Mr Logie said he never saw his friend again,' I remind them both.

'Old Logie has been really rotten,' remarks Melanie.

We shouldn't blame Mr Logie. He's trying to protect us, especially me.

It's my fault Jonty has got trapped in Spinney Wood. If it wasn't for me, none of this would have happened. So that means it's up to me to try and rescue him.

I remember Uncle Steven's advice to follow my hunches.

I'm going back to Spinney Wood.

But this time, I'm going alone.

*

As soon as school ends, I make my way past the last house on the estate before winding my way round the back of the wood on the north side of Spinney Wood. It's about as far away from the road as you can be, and the sound of traffic fades.

The trees are soaked from a late afternoon shower, and tiny droplets of water fall off some of the leaves. It's getting colder as the low, fading sun dips beyond the horizon. Occasionally, a crumpled leaf spins gently to the forest floor.

A threadbare dirt track runs for fifty yards. I pass a few spindly trees that are dotted on either side of the track until a large and unwieldy thicket begins to obstruct the route.

Leaden clouds drift across the wood. The stillness makes my senses sharper.

The slightest rustle of a branch or the sound of a bird is amplified. The ground is wet and smells of sodden wood. The dampness seeps through my skin and makes me shiver.

The trees start to dance and sway. They jostle each other, whispering to tell one another I'm here.

'I can do this, I can do this,' I mutter. My breath comes in short, sharp bursts. I pause, hoping to see some sign that I'm close to where I saw her.

The sound of rustling leaves suddenly breaks the silence. A green bush beside me rubs its leaves together.

A dull, throbbing sound reverberates around the ground. It's getting louder.

I step forward and stop in my tracks. Between the green mangled undergrowth, a dazzling pair of eyes meets my gaze. This time, I see the face clearly. There's a white sheen over it, as if cobwebs are etched into the skin.

Everything is perfectly still.

Slowly, the silken threads fall away from the face, as if a light wind has blown them off. The forehead is heavily lined with deep furrows. It's a face wizened with age, although it's difficult to tell how old. The eyelids open. They're soft and welcoming.

I move tentatively forward and take a big breath.

The rustling of the leaves crescendos, making my body tingle.

The boughs of the trees wave their arms in a frenzy. It feels like they're rushing towards me.

The eyes are magnets, pulling me onwards with their pure light.

They blink slowly, which catches me off guard, and my heart skips a beat.

Time stands still.

Slowly, I inch forward.

The wood seems to have vanished. I feel gripped by a force, pulling me towards the face – the woman.

Suddenly the tangled undergrowth throws back its mass of seething foliage, revealing something quite extraordinary.

It's simply magical.

TWENTY

The air is warm, like a thick blanket wrapped around me, and the dampness of the wood has gone.

The sun is shining, which doesn't make sense, as it was sinking behind the horizon in the wood.

Something has changed.

The bright sky stretches for miles and it's incredibly sunny. Rich, vibrant grass covers the field, running down to the bottom of a valley. A gentle splash of water tumbles over some rocks.

The trees have thick, silvery barks, their branches spreading in every direction. Even their leaves have a glossy shine to them.

To the left of the field is a lake. Canoes and pedaloes are tied up at a landing stage.

Midway across the lake is a bridge, and to the left is a massive play area. A dirt track circles the perimeter. I suddenly wish I had a BMX.

Treehouses are dotted around the tops of trees. There are bridges made of logs running between them, like wooden pathways.

I spot children playing football down in the valley. Others are watching the game.

It's like no other place I've ever seen.

Suddenly a stooped, hooded figure steps out of the darkened shadows to greet me.

'Michael.'

The voice is croaky. The face is hidden, angled away from me.

I can tell by the voice that it's a woman.

She appears, shuffling slowly towards me, bent double, gripping a staff in one hand. She stops in front of me.

As she opens her mouth, her sore-ridden gums reveal blackened teeth.

I can hear myself breathing hard, and wait anxiously for whatever might happen. Her breath is rancid. I step backwards.

She's small, even smaller than me. I watch her closely as she throws back the brown hood of her tattered cloak. Her grey matted hair is knotted and covers most of her scrawny, drawn face.

She lifts her head and her eyes lock on me. I freeze. She circles around me. Slowly.

I'm trying to concentrate on my breathing and show her I'm not afraid. Except I am.

'Moteo,' she hisses.

'M… M… Moteo?' I stutter. 'That's your name?'

I can see her face completely now; thin strands of silk are laced across her sallow features. I try not to look too closely, but can't help noticing the spiders criss-crossing her skin. She stops circling me.

Her breathing is wheezy, and saliva drips out of her chapped lips, like rancid honey.

The luminous eyes are like shafts of pure light.

I take a step away, averting my eyes to the fields below. The children are still playing football, while others are sprawled out in the short grass, enjoying the sunshine.

I summon a deep breath. I have to search for Jonty.

With a sudden movement, she reaches for my hand.

I wrench my arm away. I need to find Jonty now – and get out of here.

She must have read my mind because she suddenly screeches, 'Jonty!'

She raises an arm, which causes her to grimace.

Her eyes dazzle as a portly figure slowly ambles up the hill, towards us. He swaggers from side to side, as if it's too much effort.

The gentle incline gives me an uninterrupted view.

I start to feel the familiar panic I used to get, right before every time Jonty would give me a knuckle sandwich.

My hands are shaking and I swallow hard as I get ready to meet Jonty.

He stops short of where I'm standing and sizes me

up. He plants his legs firmly apart, moving within a whisker of my face.

'Haven't got anyone to save you today, squirt.' He grins.

'I don't know what I'm supposed to have done. I can't help who I am. I just get anxious about things and people,' I say, frustration mingled with fear.

Moteo looks on.

'Don't think Moteo will help you, Dobbin,' Jonty says.

My breathing slows down as I realise he'll do whatever he wants to do to me anyway. So, what's the point?

He grabs my neck and whips my legs from under me. I wince as my shoulder crashes to the ground.

'Don't forget it was me that brought you here, Jonty,' I splutter.

'So what? You want a medal, stable boy?' He pinches my nose tightly.

Jonty presses his knees on my shoulders, causing me to wince.

I crane my neck and see Moteo hovering nearby.

She moves slowly around me. I close my eyes and concentrate on Jonty. A shiver runs through my body, like a bony finger running down my spine.

Moteo stoops to whisper into my ear. 'Family,' is all she says. A thin cackle escapes from her slimy mouth. And a slow, simmering smile creases her face.

My head feels fuzzy, and I'm unable to think

straight. I screw my eyes tight and try to focus on why I'm here.

Jonty starts to stuff grass into my mouth with one hand. He flicks my ears with his other.

'I know! I know how you take children!' I say, spewing grass out of my mouth.

I say it loudly enough for Moteo to hear.

'What you talking about, horsey boy?' says a puzzled Jonty.

'Enough!' Moteo shouts at Jonty, waving her gnarled hand in our direction. She leers at me and I quickly look away. I shake uncontrollably when I see her eyes.

Jonty slowly removes one knee, and then the other, from my aching shoulders.

He looks at Moteo sheepishly, and gets up. Without a second glance at me, he lumbers down the slope and towards the other children.

I get shakily to my feet.

'J... J... Jonty shouldn't be here,' I stammer, forcing the words out.

'Oath binds,' Moteo says, her steely stare holding me.

'What oath?' I ask.

She suddenly feigns sadness. 'My family... is gone.' She slowly shakes her head.

'This is now my family.' She extends her hand to the children below.

She's replaced her own family with all these missing children!

She lifts her head upwards to the towering trees. I

sense the trees are laughing at me! How is that possible?

'Curse!' she hisses. A raucous laugh leaves her mouth.

Ben's words come into my mind. 'The curse of Spinney Wood!'

The trees suddenly swoop down, their long branches reaching out like the arms of an octopus.

I step back as Moteo cackles quietly.

Suddenly I feel drained of all energy and my head is swimming. All I want to do is sleep.

I blink hard and rub my hands over my eyes. I need to go… now… is all I can think.

I take a deep breath and avert my eyes from Moteo's gaze as I stumble past her.

She raises a withered arm. 'Bye bye,' is all she says.

Gathering speed, I run through the archway and into the tangled undergrowth. I flail my arms, eyes partly closed, trying to find a way through. Suddenly I realise I'm sweeping through fresh air.

I've come out the other side.

I shiver as the dampness of Spinney Wood hits me.

Quickly moving through the wood, I can't stop to think about what's just happened.

What did she mean about a curse?

I'm pretty sure Mr Logie knows, but he obviously doesn't want to speak to me. Worse than that, I'm sure I've made him ill. Really ill.

TWENTY-ONE

'What time do you call this?' cries Mum, as she races up from the dining-room table and flings her arms around me.

She's sobbing quietly, and her tears are rolling against my face as I nervously look over at Dad, who's standing near the fireplace.

There's a police officer sitting at the table.

'I was so worried.' Her face is blotchy, and red. She steps back to take a better look at me.

'Sorry, I should have rung,' I say.

I quickly check my face in the lounge mirror. I take a breath to assess how I'm feeling. I feel okay. Surprisingly.

'Michael, we thought something had happened,' Dad says. He's home from work early, following Mum's frantic phone call.

'Look at your shoes, they're all muddy,' says Mum, glancing down at the trail of dirt I've brought into the house. 'I'll give them an extra clean tonight. Where on earth have you been?' she says.

I choose not to answer. 'Where's Uncle Steven?' I ask instead. He's usually in the lounge when I get home. 'He's not gone back to his own place yet, surely?'

'Can you just listen to what we're saying!' says Mum.

'I suppose the most important thing is that you're safe,' the police officer says calmly.

This seems to break the tension, and we all nod in agreement. I release my tensed shoulders and exhale a huge sigh of relief.

'So… you want to tell us where you've been, Michael?' the police officer says, almost casually, putting his notebook away.

Mum is dabbing at her wet cheeks with a tissue. She gestures towards me, telling me to respond.

'A walk, that's all. What's the big deal? It's not that late,' I say quietly.

'That's not the point!' Mum shouts. 'I was worried.'

I sigh. 'Well, there was no need to be. I didn't think, that's all, about ringing, I mean.'

'Sorry,' says Mum, smiling at the police officer. 'We get so worried about Michael.'

'With everything going on with that boy Jonty's disappearance, well, we're all a bit on edge,' adds Dad.

Mum gives Dad a withering look. 'I'm at my wits' end,' she says, holding her head.

'We're *both* worried,' Dad says.

'Don't suppose you can say too much about what's happening with the Jonty case?' says Dad to the police officer.

'Still ongoing,' the police officer gives a polite smile, 'but these young people do need to be careful. Never can be too safe,' he says, and eyeballs me.

'I expect his mum's beside herself with worry,' Mum continues, 'but, and I don't like to say this… but between you and me, they didn't get on that well.' She lowers her voice to a whisper.

Dad shoots her a warning glance.

The police officer keeps zip. He turns to me.

'Now then, young Michael, next time, let your mum know where you are, right?' He picks up his helmet.

I nod and breathe a sigh of relief – no more questions. At least from the police.

'Hope you find the lad,' says Dad, and shows the police officer to the front door.

As soon the door is closed, Mum steps right in front of me and puts her face within inches of mine.

I keep my head down but can feel her hot breath all over my skin.

'Do you have any idea what you've put me through, Michael? I've been worried sick wondering where you were!' she cries.

'Leave him alone, Debs. That's not going to help now, is it!' Dad says.

'What would you know? You're never here most of

the time,' Mum snaps back.

'Why are you arguing?' I ask. 'I was okay.'

'I'm not sure what's got into you lately, Michael,' says Dad, sinking into an armchair. 'You've been behaving very strangely recently.'

'Look at your shoes! You've been to Spinney Wood again, after everything I've said. I can't believe it,' Mum says, pointing at my wet and muddied shoes.

I couldn't deny it.

'Leave finding your friend to the police,' warns Dad.

'He's not my friend. Why would you think he's my friend? Anyway, the police don't have a clue, do they?'

Mum shoots me a quizzical look.

'What do you mean?'

'They're doing all they can. It's early days,' Dad says. 'Why don't you leave all this alone and just do normal stuff, like other lads of your age?'

Mum shakes her head and bites her lip.

'So, Michael…' Mum glares at me. 'You think you know better than the police, is that it?'

'What if I do?' I retort.

'I expect it's that Mr Logie again who's put you up to this,' she says. 'I'm definitely going to speak to him at parents' evening. He's so irresponsible.' Mum reaches for her notebook and pen.

'As if that's going to help!' Dad says, and laughs gruffly.

I can't listen to this any longer. It's making my head pound. I need to escape to my bedroom.

'Is Uncle Steven resting?' I look towards his bedroom.

They don't seem bothered about answering my questions about Uncle Steven!

'It's just not normal, he's always talking about Spinney Wood and its "interesting history". She makes quote marks in the air with her fingers when she says *interesting history*, mocking Mr Logie.

'What do you mean anyway, that you know more than the police?' Dad asks.

I ignore him, rush down the hallway and knock on Uncle Steven's door.

Silence.

'Where's Uncle Steven?' I ask. I feel a sense of rising panic.

Mum looks twitchy.

'He had to leave,' she says.

'I thought you said he was here till tomorrow?' I say, surprised.

'He started to feel unwell, so I had to call an ambulance,' Mum replies, eyeing me warily.

'Why, what's wrong?' She's not telling me everything.

'He's been having problems lately. He's finding it difficult to… to control himself sometimes,' Mum says, looking away.

'Control himself?' I repeat anxiously.

Dad gets up and starts to walk out of the room.

'He is all right, though, yeah?' I ask.

Dad looks back at me with some sympathy. 'They

told us to ring the hospital in a few hours. Probably after they've done tests,' he says.

'Why is Uncle Steven in a wheelchair, Mum?'

She heaves a big sigh and lowers herself into the armchair. She taps her fingers on the fabric.

'He fell out of a tree, when we were young,' she says calmly.

Her face is pale, the colour drained from her cheeks. She pauses, deep in thought. Then, she continues. 'We had a huge beech tree at the bottom of our garden near the fields. My dad built a treehouse for us there. We used to spend hours hiding in it. It was fun.' She gives a weak smile.

Dad halts at the door as Mum carries on.

'One day, I thought I'd go up a bit higher, up to the next big branch, just to see what the view was like. We could see for miles,' she recalls.

I have a horrible feeling I know where this story is heading.

'So I did.' She shrugs her shoulders. 'But I couldn't get down.' A frown clouds her face. 'Steven came to rescue me,' she says quietly.

Dad's stony face has started to soften.

'I made it down safely.' She buries her head and starts to cry again.

'Thing is, he never complains, or *blames*,' says Dad.

'I've hated being near trees ever since,' Mum cries. 'You don't need to be up there in Spinney Wood,' she sniffles. 'You're just putting yourself in danger, Michael.'

'He'll be all right, won't he? Uncle Steven?' I say desperately.

But Mum's lost in her childhood memories.

TWENTY-TWO

I'm in the main hall, down from Mr Jones' classroom, and I'm still thinking about how Uncle Steven is. I can't get him out of my mind. He's probably attached to lots of machines with wires and tubes coming out of his body. The hospital said it was too early to give any definite answers.

Maybe we can visit later.

Students are heading into classrooms off the main corridor for registration. At the end of the corridor, I spy a police officer talking to Mr Yates.

Mr Yates has his arms behind his back and is bouncing up on his toes.

They're shaking hands now and smiling. I wonder what that was all about.

I'm still in the habit of keeping an eye on the swing doors at the end of the corridor. They lead out to the playground. That's where Jonty would hang about ready to 'greet' me in his usual unfriendly manner.

I wander into Mr Jones' classroom.

Melanie and Ben are already at their desks.

Melanie leans over. 'Where did you go yesterday?'

'I had to see if Jonty was still in Spinney Wood,' I say. 'Guess what! I saw him and Moteo!'

'Who?' quizzes Melanie.

'Moteo, that's her name, the tribal woman. The one who's been taking all those children that have gone missing.'

Melanie stares at me for what seems like ages.

'Honest!' I plead.

'So what happened?' she asks.

'Well, Jonty is still angry with me for starters,' I admit.

'Okay, well, listen to this…' Melanie looks round to make sure no one overhears. 'I went round to the address, the one from the newspaper cutting.'

'I went as well,' Ben reminds Melanie.

'What!' I mouth my disbelief.

'So I knocked on the door and this woman answered. I said I was doing a school project about all the missing children. To raise awareness, you know, that sort of thing.'

That's trespassing, I think.

'She was so sad.' Melanie looks genuinely upset. 'Her son Robert used to live there with her, before he disappeared,' she says, biting her lip.

'She said *Robert*?' I ask.

'Yes,' confirms Melanie. 'Funny thing was, she showed me a gap on the wall where a framed photo was missing. She got really upset about it because it was the last one she had of her and Robert before he disappeared.'

I watch Melanie's furrowed brow as she reflects on what she's just said.

'There were loads of photographs on the wall, and they were all...' She pauses.

'Like the one in Mr Logie's briefcase!' I finish her thought.

Melanie nods slowly. 'That's when I left,' she says.

'I made an excuse to go to the bathroom and saw one of the bedroom doors open,' says Ben. 'So I had a quick peek.'

I look shocked.

'There were football posters and famous players on the wall. Looked like they were all wearing the Dutch football kit,' says Ben.

I shake my head in disbelief.

'What?' he says. 'I was just being a good detective,' he defends himself.

'So what's the connection between Mr Logie and this family?'

But there's no more time to carry on our conversation, as Mr Jones has started to read out registration. He calls out Jonty's name by mistake, and an uncomfortable silence descends on the class.

After registration, we head off to Mr Yates' maths class.

I struggle to compare the decimals and calculations as the numbers just jump around and won't stay on the paper.

I check my phone in case Mum has updated me about Uncle Steven.

Nothing.

It's nearly the end of the day.

Collecting a few books from my locker, I spy the familiar figure of Mr Logie hovering outside his classroom.

I collect my books and hurry along to see him. Just to see if he's all right.

'Michael, what are you doing here?' he says cheerfully.

I'm sure his hair has turned slightly greyer. His furrowed brow has more creases.

I rock from side to side but carry on. 'I thought you weren't very well, sir. We were told you were off sick for a few days.'

'Sick?' he repeats. 'I don't think so.'

But he does looks slightly frail, I think.

'Sorry if I upset you last time we spoke, sir,' I say.

He looks at me blankly.

'Did you?' he says, puzzled.

He looks really confused.

'Sorry, Michael, can't stay to chat. I've got some

packing to do,' he says, looking up and down the corridor. 'Need to leave at the end of the day.'

'But sir...' I begin.

He ignores me and walks into his classroom. His tattered briefcase is on the table. His desk is clear. The league tables have disappeared off the wall.

I'm going to try something.

'Robert?' I ask.

His jaw drops and I notice the shadows under his eyes. It looks like he hasn't slept much recently.

'Sir, I am right, aren't I? That was your name?' I push on.

He glances towards the ceiling. 'Yes, I believe it was,' he says sadly.

'What you said about the wood and its history is true, sir, isn't it, sir? You were right all along,' I say, trying to encourage him.

His eyes look vacant as he removes his orange scarf off one of the doors. A few threads are missing.

'Is that your scarf from your days in Amsterdam, sir?' I ask.

Mr Logie frowns and nods his head. 'Yes, good days they were, on the whole. I even watched a few matches. How did you know that, Michael?' he asks.

But he doesn't wait for an answer.

'Look, I'm sorry you've got involved, Michael. I did try to stop you.' There's desperation in his voice.

Mr Logie puts on his coat and scarf, picks up his briefcase, a few other boxes and leaves.

'I want to help, sir,' I call out to him.

He stops and shakes his head. 'No, Michael,' he says firmly. 'I need to go now,' he says.

He hesitates as he goes out the door, as though he's forgotten something. But then with a shake of his head he carries on and leaves.

TWENTY-THREE

The three of us are having lunch in the school canteen. I don't feel hungry. I can't believe Mum's put another almond bar in my lunch box.

There's still no news about Uncle Steven.

Mum rang the hospital and he's had a peaceful night. The doctors will look at him today.

'Bit of a coincidence?' says Melanie. 'Mr Logie, Amsterdam, the footie pictures on the wall. Don't you think?'

'The missing photograph at that woman's house,' pipes Ben.

I think back to the newspaper in Mr Logie's briefcase. That unmistakable beak.

A couple of tables away near the back of the canteen, I watch Harrison devouring his second doughnut. He's got jam all over his mouth.

Pierce nearly falls off his chair as he tries to avoid a stray squirt of jam that splatters on his trousers.

He clips Harrison with his hand around the ear. They throw part of their drinks over each other, much to the amusement of the rest of the dining area. There's a steady trickle of food and drink flowing under their table, to which they seem oblivious.

I suddenly wish I could swap places with Harrison or Pierce.

They bounce from one thing to the next, without a care in the world. They take the rough with the smooth. Nothing seems to bother them.

'Michael, what about this plan of ours?' says Melanie, snapping her fingers in front of my face.

'*Ours*?' I say.

'Well, we came up with zilch last time,' says Ben. 'So, what's the new plan?' He looks at me optimistically.

One of the canteen staff turns chairs upside down on the tables as they clear up. Another lady is mopping the floor.

'But you've been in there, Michael,' Melanie reminds me.

I get it.

'It's up to *me*, not *us*. The trees knew I wasn't on my own. It's only me that's allowed to enter… that place,' I say, casting my gaze to the floor.

'But Jonty got in there with you,' Melanie starts. 'Perhaps we could get in the same way as Jonty?'

'You mean we can all be Time Lords?' cries Ben, mouth wide open.

Maybe Melanie has a point and there might be a way we can all go through the portal. 'Okay. Well, I'm not sure, but we've got to do something, haven't we?' I say. 'We need to give it one more go, if you're both up for it?'

'Ace! Don't suppose I can bring Jasper again?' asks Ben.

Melanie and I laugh.

TWENTY-FOUR

When I arrive home from school, Mum is in the kitchen, busy filling a bag. In go two cartons of orange juice, a big bunch of grapes and a large box of tissues.

'We're going to see Uncle Steven,' she announces.

'Oh, how is he?' I ask.

'Your dad is coming home early. We'll eat later.'

She didn't answer my question.

Mum seems on edge. She checks all the doors are locked.

I suddenly remember the meeting they went to. The one with the counsellor. 'How was your meeting?' I ask.

'We've got another one in a couple of weeks,' she replies, and offers me a fixed smile.

'So, is everything all right between you and Dad?' I ask.

'We're just having a difficult time at the moment,' she says carefully, lowering her gaze.

'It's because of me, isn't it?' I slump against the door frame.

Mum puts her bag down and grabs me by the arms. 'No, no, Michael, this has nothing to do with you!' She gently shakes me. 'It's silly arguments, that's all. It'll be all right, I expect,' she says, trying to reassure me.

I'm not convinced.

I wish I could just dump all this anxiety. I know they worry about me. It's stupid spending time hiding in my room like a mole. Or suddenly getting wound up and going off like Jack Flash.

I sling my rucksack on the sofa and crash down beside it. I don't care about dinner being later. Not that hungry anyway.

Mum moves into the lounge and takes a long look out of the window.

She stretches her neck to look up and down the street before drawing the blinds.

'Really, there's nothing to worry about,' Mum says, smiling. She holds my head gently and plants a kiss on my forehead. 'I think we all need to change,' she says softly.

'I'll get out of my school things,' I say, and start to get up.

'No, we haven't got time,' Mum states. 'We won't be long anyway,' she replies.

If Mum could drive, we could go straight to the hospital now without waiting for Dad.

Dad arrives ten minutes later and thirty minutes after that we're at the hospital.

I hate the smell of hospitals. They have that peculiar smell of disinfectant, a bit like our house when Mum's on a cleaning binge.

Mum clenches her fists tightly and we head for reception. Dad looks straight ahead as we stop and get directions for Uncle Steven's ward. It's not that busy. We march down the long white corridors.

They haven't said much to each other on the way here.

A few patients pass by, wheeled in chairs by relatives or on beds pushed by hospital porters. It's all a bit gloomy. I get it. People are ill. Everyone looks so sombre. Which I suppose is to be expected.

We reach the ward and use the hand gel on the wall to sanitise our hands. There are a couple of nurses sitting behind a desk. One of them is writing. There's also someone pushing a tea trolley.

Mum wanders further into the ward. She glances at each patient in turn until we recognise Uncle Steven.

We gather around him and Mum draws the curtains around his bed.

He's half-asleep. He looks odd in those stripy hospital pyjamas.

Dad clears his throat and Uncle Steven stirs.

'Hi, mate, how you doing?' Dad asks cheerfully.

Uncle Steven feigns surprise and a whimpering sound escapes. 'Oh, you know, can't complain,' he whispers.

Mum raises her eyes and attempts a smile.

There's stubble on Uncle Steven's chin.

'I brought you some orange juice and grapes,' Mum says, holding up the bag.

'Thanks,' Uncle Steven replies. But he doesn't reach out to take them.

Mum puts the grapes and juice on his table at the end of the bed, for him to have later.

'So, what have the doctors said?' Mum asks.

'Compression on the spinal cord,' he states without flinching. 'Wear and tear, I'm afraid.'

Mum looks stricken.

'They'll have the physio working on you soon, I reckon,' Dad pipes up. He looks at Mum with hopeful eyes.

Uncle Steven lifts his hands and grimaces. 'She'll have her work cut out with me,' he says, but he's smiling now.

He turns his head to focus on me. 'How're you doing, my man?'

'Fine,' but I can't stop looking at all the wires and tubes dotted around his bed.

'What about your mates, Melanie and Ben?' he asks.

'They're good,' I say.

He seems to be struggling to swallow and smacks his dry lips together. Mum pours some water into a plastic cup.

'Here, drink this,' she says.

She lifts his head with one hand, and tips the cup to meet his mouth.

Water dribbles down his chin. 'What am I like?' he splutters. 'Need a bib soon,' he jokes.

He starts to cough and it's difficult for him to clear his throat. He closes his eyes and sinks back into the pillow.

A nurse appears. Mum and I move slightly away to allow her to come alongside Uncle Steven.

'Everything all right, Steven?' she says briskly. She plumps up his pillows and lays his head down gently. She checks his pulse and the readings on the computer next to his bed. Then, seemingly satisfied, she heads back to the nurses' station.

'He's tired,' says Mum, which is our cue to leave. 'Night, Steven. Get a good night's rest,' she says.

Uncle Steven's eyes are closed and he doesn't reply.

As we walk down the corridor, I ask Mum, 'What do you think will happen?'

'We'll have to see,' she says, giving my arm a quick squeeze.

I glance up at Dad. He's trying to hold himself together.

Follow your hunches, Uncle Steven said.

Jack Flash is on the case.

I'll make Uncle Steven proud.

TWENTY-FIVE

Back at school the next day, I catch up with Melanie and Ben as they're walking down the corridor.

I notice Miss Pearson is busy talking to Mr Yates at the bottom of the stairwell. It's quite dark underneath the stairs that lead to the science rooms.

They're huddled together with their backs to us. A third person is trying to get past them. Mr Yates and Miss Pearson are restraining them.

I alert Melanie and Ben to the struggle. We move stealthily over to where the scene is unfolding.

We duck in behind a row of lockers.

It's another man. Smaller than the imposing figure of Mr Yates, who is now forcibly holding on to the other man.

The stairwell leads to a dead end at the end of this corridor. There's no classrooms, only the maintenance room where all the cleaning and other equipment is kept. If he escapes, he'll have to get past them and us, on the way out.

We all move over to one of the exit doors next to the playground. We can get a better view from there.

Suddenly the man breaks free of Mr Yates' grip. An orange scarf falls to the floor in the struggle.

'I need to see him!' the man shouts. He sounds quite distressed.

Miss Pearson is trying to quieten him down.

'You're not well,' she says soothingly.

'Go home and get some rest, David,' suggests Mr Yates.

'I *can't* rest,' he cries. 'Not until I see Michael.'

'Mr Logie! Look, it's him!' I hiss.

'Goodness, I'd hardly have recognised him,' Melanie whispers back.

Mr Logie has a little bit of stubble on his chin. He looks slightly dishevelled.

I step out to the top of the stairwell. Mr Logie peers around Mr Yates' imposing figure and spots me.

'Michael!' he yells.

Mr Yates swivels round and signals for me to leave.

It must be embarrassing for Mr Logie. Anguish spreads across his face. He's not a lot like our history teacher at the minute.

Miss Pearson puts a holding arm on Mr Yates, who lessens his firm grip.

'I need to talk to you, Michael. I remembered I need to tell you something!' Mr Logie cries.

Mr Yates releases his grip on Mr Logie, who takes a step back. But he doesn't run away.

Melanie, Ben and I move over to get closer as Mr Yates turns to speak to me.

'Between you and me, Mr Logie is having… a sort of breakdown, I'm afraid,' he says, and frowns.

Mr Logie lifts his hands, trying to convince the teachers he won't cause any trouble.

'I'm all right, honest,' he says, shaking himself down. 'I just need to have a quick word with Michael, then I'll be off,' he tells Mr Yates.

'Mmm, so be it,' says Mr Yates, shaking his head.

He nods towards Mr Logie and straightens his jacket.

Miss Pearson whispers to me as she passes. 'Gardening leave for a while, I'm afraid,' she confides. 'He keeps mumbling about a portal or something!'

I can't believe they don't know he's ill. They're not listening!

Mr Yates and Miss Pearson head off back down the corridor together.

Melanie, Ben and I move down the steps and duck under the stairwell, which is gloomy but quiet. It's away from any onlookers.

Mr Logie slumps against the wall.

I carefully study his face. It looks more stretched and pale. He looks so unwell!

'My friends are still in there!' he says tearfully.

'Friends?' I ask.

I've never seen an adult cry.

We all look at one another, not sure what to do or say.

'It happens,' he says breathlessly, 'when Moteo's energy is low. She steals a child,' he gasps. 'On the date of the massacre, the portal opens.'

'You were the boy in the newspaper, weren't you, sir, all those years ago?' I ask.

There is a moment's silence, then Mr Logie looks up, his lip quivering.

'Yes, it was me in Spinney Wood,' he admits forlornly.

'Mr Yates called you David, but your real name is Robert, isn't it?' I say.

'I changed my name when I left. Made a fresh start, where nobody knew me, or the secret of Spinney Wood,' he adds.

'So you moved abroad,' Melanie says.

'You went to Amsterdam,' Ben says.

'Yes, I did, for a while. But then I heard it was happening more often. Not every year, but I couldn't sit idly by while other children went through what I went through,' Mr Logie says, despair filling his voice.

'Her world is old, ancient by most standards.' He hesitates. 'She's getting desperate now. Her energy levels are getting weaker.'

'That's why I could get in,' says Michael.

A deep sigh leaves me.

'You were in the wrong place at the wrong time,' he says to me, almost in the way of an apology.

'Bit like child sacrifice…' whispers Ben.

'She hated me at the end. Not at first, of course. She's welcoming. You are part of her family.' He forces a chuckle. 'But she soon changes. I remembered the date I was taken. So I simply watched and waited. The portal opens on that exact day.'

I watch his eyes flicker nervously at the memory.

'So if the portal only opens on the day of the massacre, it means we can't get in again,' reasons Melanie.

'That's not all.' He casts a forlorn look at each of us in turn.

'What is it?' I ask.

'She said I was under a curse.' There's real fear in Mr Logie's eyes now.

'Curse?' asks Ben, glancing nervously at me. 'Wh… wh… what kind of curse?'

'I saw her, sir, Moteo, that is, in Spinney Wood. She said something about a curse,' I butt in.

'Moteo thinks her secret is safe,' Mr Logie says with resignation.

'Curse, sir? You were going to say something about a curse,' says Ben persistently.

He wipes a tear from his eyes. 'I had to tell someone, you understand,' he says. 'It shouldn't be happening—'

'But the secret must never be shared,' I interject. 'That's it, isn't it?'

'That's right,' says Mr Logie sadly.

'Why?' asks Melanie.

Mr Logie's face droops to one side. His thin, ashen face begins to shrivel as he struggles to control his emotions.

'Because, if I share her secret, then this happens.' He points to his rapidly ageing face.

We all gasp in unison.

'I think you need to see a doctor, sir, before it's too late,' I say. He looks as if he can barely stand now.

A faint smile flickers across his face. 'Doctor? I think it's too late for a doctor. And it's too late for most of the children in there too. She keeps them alive, well beyond their years,' he says.

He begins to sway gently. Melanie reaches out a hand to steady him.

'But there are younger children – those that have disappeared recently. They can be saved, can't they? Children like Jonty. That's why you came back, sir, wasn't it?' I raise my voice.

Melanie raises her eyebrows. 'Why didn't you say something earlier – stopped more children disappearing?'

Mr Logie hangs his head. 'I'm so sorry,' he says.

'But the secret's out now, sir,' I say softly.

'Yes, Michael, it's out. That's the problem,' Mr Logie says sadly. 'That's why a doctor can't help me. Or you. The curse is binding. It devours you. You just waste away and then…'

Ben moves his head forward in anticipation of what Mr Logie is about to say.

'What can we do then?' Melanie almost shouts in frustration.

I put a hand out to restrain her.

Mr Logie slowly turns his head to Melanie and smiles. 'Nothing. Everyone's trapped,' he says, his soft voice barely audible.

'Crikey! That means you've been cursed, a real curse!' says Ben, backing away from me.

I glance up at Melanie as I suddenly realise what this means.

That's it. It's over. For Jonty, Mr Logie. The other children. And me.

I'm going to get ill too.

Melanie and Ben look at me in a way which gives me the creeps.

Mr Logie leaves the stairwell and slowly climbs the steps. He glances over his shoulder. 'I'm afraid it's a battle you can't win, Michael. Sorry, but I did try and warn you – all of you.'

Melanie, Ben and I stand silent for a few moments. Then Melanie pipes up in her usual brisk, businesslike manner. 'Don't worry, Michael. We'll think of something. There must be something we can do. If we all put our heads together, including you, Ben Gillet... for what it's worth,' she adds, winking at him.

'Reason, boys and girls, is your greatest friend,' booms Ben.

I feel the warmth of their friendship; it calms me.

'Well, let's see, boy, what evidence do we have?' Ben continues, in a deep voice, mimicking Mr Yates. His head bobs up and down like a demented meerkat.

I laugh out loud. Thankfully, Mr Yates is no longer in the corridor to hear him.

We watch Mr Logie staggering down the corridor, holding on to the wall for support.

'He looks like a hundred years old,' Ben muses.

I swallow hard. 'The curse is eating away at him. It'll only get worse.'

'Do you think he'll make it home?' Melanie says.

'I'm not sure he'll make it to the end of the corridor,' Ben replies.

'We can't let Mr Logie die!' I shout.

I'm surprised how confident I feel. There's no sign of either Mole or Jack Flash.

It's just me – Michael Dobson!

I feel good about myself for the first time in years.

TWENTY-SIX

We race down the corridor and try to catch up with Mr Logie as he wobbles towards the swing doors and staggers through the main exit.

Miss Pearson is standing on the large patio outside the doors, making sure everyone leaves in an orderly fashion.

'Make sure you get yourself well, David,' she calls to him.

Mr Yates joins her, shaking his head as Mr Logie lumbers towards the bike shed.

'He's going to cycle? Like that? No way!' says Ben, watching him.

'He'll have an accident!' exclaims Melanie.

We reach him as he's fumbling to open the lock on his bike. I grab his arm and pull him gently away from his bike. Melanie takes his other arm and we guide him towards a low wall. His legs shake with every step.

We lower him down gently on the wall while he gets his breath back.

'I'm not as young as I used to be,' he says, sucking in a deep breath.

'He can't go home by himself,' I say, loudly enough to shame Mr Yates, who's standing idly by.

There's only one thing to do.

I get my phone out and call Mum.

'Mum, can you come and pick Mr Logie up from school?' I plead.

I'm aware of how odd my request is, but hope she notices the urgency in my voice.

It's a long shot, I know. Mum doesn't like driving. She hasn't driven in years.

'It's an emergency,' I stress. 'Please, hurry up, and drive to school.'

I'm not leaving this spot until Mr Logie is safe! I say as much to Mum.

There's a long silence at the end of the line.

Then she finally agrees.

The school is now deserted apart from the caretaker, who's looking at us uneasily from behind the glass windows.

'You don't need to wait,' I tell Melanie and Ben. 'I can take things from here.'

Melanie and Ben both give me a really weird look.

'We'll wait,' Melanie says calmly.

I bend over to check on Mr Logie. His breathing is quite laboured.

'My mum's coming to give you a lift,' I reassure him.

'Perhaps it's time I saw *my* mother,' he says, smiling. 'She's not getting any younger.'

'She'd like that, I expect,' says Melanie, and exchanges a look of concern with me.

'You're going back, aren't you, Michael? To the woods?' Mr Logie says weakly.

I speak clearly and firmly. 'Yes.'

'The *three* of you?' he asks, looking intently into first Melanie's eyes and then Ben's.

Melanie lowers her gaze and sucks in her cheeks.

Ben nods, although I know his brain hasn't quite worked out what that means.

'You don't have to come,' I say to Melanie and Ben. 'It's me she really wants,' I say. I chew my bottom lip.

'What? And miss being a Time Lord!' Ben says, bouncing up and down. 'Anyway, you need someone with a bit of imagination!'

'And someone who can use their logic!' adds Melanie. 'Cos, let's face it, Ben's not exactly made friends with logic, have you, Ben?' Melanie cocks her head sideways and gives Ben one of her withering looks.

'I'll check him out on Facebook.' Ben pulls a funny face back at her.

'Imagination and logic…' ponders Mr Logie.

'First thing's first,' I say confidently, 'we need to get Mr Logie home. Then we need to find a way to stop all this bad stuff that's happening in Spinney Wood… and rescue Jonty,' I add as an afterthought.

I feel quite proud just saying it like that.

'Oh yes, I remember now,' Mr Logie splutters. 'The portal opens on the anniversary of the battle.'

'Yes, you said, sir. That's how you escaped, sir, wasn't it, all those years ago?' I ask.

'And it stays open for as long as the battle lasted... ten days...' he says.

'That's why I could get in a second time when I saw Jonty,' I say.

'Wait! What day did you first go into Spinney Wood?' Melanie asks me.

My jaw drops. I do some quick sums in my head.

'Today is the tenth day!' Melanie beats me to it. 'There are only a few hours left till it closes!' she says.

'The portal closes this evening!' I say.

Ben's eyes flicker from left to right as he tries to keep up.

'I'll explain later,' Melanie says impatiently to him.

Mr Logie is very dozy now. He rests against my shoulder as I prop him up.

A few minutes later, I spy Mum turning carefully into the driveway. She is hunched over the steering wheel, her face nearly touching the windscreen. She is one careful driver!

She finally comes to a halt and I wave at her.

I push Mr Logie towards Melanie and he flops against her.

Mum gets out of the car and looks at Mr Logie slumped against Melanie.

'Is he drunk?' she exclaims.

'Of course he isn't,' I say.

I feel pumped. We need to be off. I just want Mum to take Mr Logie home.

'He certainly shouldn't be teaching in that state, that's for sure,' she says.

Mum's mood suddenly changes as she makes eye contact with both Melanie and Ben.

'Well, aren't you going to introduce me, Michael?' She puts on her posh voice.

'This is Melanie, Ben.' I wave my hand in their direction.

'I've heard so much about you both,' Mum says.

She stretches out her hand.

'I hear you're in the history club together,' she gushes.

I cringe, cutting her off. We haven't time for this.

'Please, Mum, we've got to go. Can you take Mr Logie home?'

'What? Where are you going?' she asks.

I choose to ignore her question and instead give her directions to get Mr Logie home. 'I think he lives in Grimshaw Street. I've seen him in his garden. Turn right at the end of the school drive, then second left. It's not far.'

'I'll never remember that.' Mum looks stressed and I feel a rush of sympathy for her. I know what it's like to feel anxious.

'I'll write it down.' Ben finds a scrap piece of paper and jots down the address.

'You haven't answered my question. Where are you going?' Mum demands.

I go to the other side of Mr Logie and we help him to his feet. He sounds very wheezy.

'Quick, open the door,' I shout to Mum.

She looks put out. But she can't back down now, especially in front of my friends.

We gently lower Mr Logie into the seat. I lift his legs into the footwell and put a seat belt on him.

Mum looks on anxiously and checks her watch. 'And tea? What about tea?'

'I'll be fine. I'm with friends,' I say, slamming the door.

I shrug my shoulders and we shoot off down the driveway.

Mum shoves Mr Logie away from her so his face is pressed against the passenger window and pulls off slowly.

Melanie, Ben and I sprint out of the school gates.

We haven't much time.

TWENTY-SEVEN

Ben has run ahead to quickly change at home. He comes back wearing his combat jacket. He's also wearing a balaclava, which makes him look like he's going to rob a bank.

He's got a lump of cheese in his hand and a crust.

'Provisions,' he says with a curt nod. 'Even Time Lords have to eat.'

'Right, I'll go into the woods first,' I say. 'The trees need to think that it's just me coming. Remember?

'You and Melanie, skirt the wood, and enter down by the farm. Moteo mustn't know you're with me.'

I can hear Uncle Steven's voice inside my head: *Inspector Dobson of the Yard!*

'You'll need to let us know when you're there. Something that won't arouse any suspicions, like a birdcall?' says Melanie.

Great idea! I can do a perfect song thrush. Even the trees will be fooled!

'Okay, then once you've heard my birdcall, join me near the archway. We can surprise Moteo if we go in together,' I say confidently.

'Make sure you have your phones on,' reminds Melanie.

Ben nods, his mouth stuffed with cheese.

'Time Lords travel on their stomachs,' he says defensively.

We split up and I watch them stride down the side of the wood, towards the farm.

I stand at the entrance to the wood and stop to study the trees. They are still. I take time to breathe a few, slow breaths, and try to find my bearings.

There's a rustle. Gentle, but perceptible. The trees huddle close together, branches stretched out, as though they're joining hands.

I know they're whispering, and passing messages to each other, as they see me approach.

The wind gathers force, and the branches sway in my direction. They seem to be pleased to see me.

The air is cold.

Suddenly a gust of wind picks up a pile of leaves and whips them into my face. A few fly into my mouth, and I spit them out. I wipe my face with an arm.

The leaves dance round my ankles in concentric circles, before dumping themselves into a pile behind me.

My legs feel like jelly. I drag myself onwards, deeper into Spinney Wood.

I start to jog, to gather speed.

My head is starting to feel muzzy.

A trickle of perspiration winds down my cheek.

Small bushes and shrubs are thrust aside as I stride through them, gritting my teeth.

I clench my fists as I stumble on, making my way into the heart of the wood.

'Ouch,' I shout, as my foot suddenly slides into a hole, covered by bracken and fallen leaves. My ankle twinges in pain. I bend down to give it a rub.

'I'm not here to hurt you!' I shout at the trees. I look up as the branches twist and bend menacingly. I suddenly feel small, and alone. I wonder if I've done the right thing.

I haven't a clue where I am. I seem to have strayed too far away from the farm.

I halt, slumping down against the base of a huge old tree. The roots are sprawled out in all directions, creating lumps in the ground.

The ground begins to vibrate as a quiet hum surrounds me. It quickly gets louder, drowning my senses.

The deep roots begin to push upwards, trying to snap away at my legs and bottom.

They're actually trying to turn me over!

The earth is swaying, and I wrap my arms around my shoulders and hold myself tight.

Thunder fills the air, and it begins to rain, lightly at first, but then much harder.

I hang my head between my knees, and water drips off my chin and onto my trousers. I cover my ears and try to block out the rumbling.

Mole is back and he wants to crawl away. I don't know what to do.

The ground stops shaking. The rain eases. I look up and wonder if any of this is right.

I drag myself up to stand. Walking to the tangled, overgrown mire of branches, thistles and dock, I see a lighted archway.

I've made it!

I fill my lungs and give the best song thrush call I can do.

Back comes another song thrush. So far, so good.

The rain suddenly stops.

And they appear – the face and the eyes.

It's time.

The eyes seem friendly, pleased to see me.

I walk over and a gap appears in the tangle of branches, making a clear path to the entrance of the archway.

I take a deep breath and creep forward. Nervously, I glance sideways to the clump of bushes, for signs of Melanie and Ben.

C'mon, guys. Surely you can't be far away!

I quickly return my gaze to the eyes. They still look welcoming.

As I take my first step through the archway and out of the gloom, I suddenly feel a tug on my blazer.

Melanie and Ben! They've made it!

Straining, I pull the three of us through into the warmth of the sunlight.

'Yes!' gushes Moteo, clasping her gnarled hands together as she spies me. She's been waiting for me to arrive. She just knew I'd be back.

She flings her arms open and commands the trees to sway. She sways gently herself, as though she's conducting an orchestra.

'Trees, good, yes,' she murmurs.

Her cracked lips are thin and purple. She beams up at the trees, drinking in their dance.

Melanie's eyes dart in every direction as she takes stock.

Ben's mouth is wide open.

Suddenly Moteo's smile vanishes as she spots Melanie and Ben.

Her sunken eyes narrow. She hisses at them both.

Melanie stands her ground, although Ben retreats a little.

Moteo has a tattered cloak thrown about her hunched shoulders.

Her grey hair is long and straight, and shines in the sun. But her complexion is sallow. A half-life not lived.

I recoil and keep my distance.

Moteo starts to circle Ben, who keeps his eyes fixed firmly on the ground.

Slowly her face changes, and a faint smile settles on her lips.

Melanie catches Ben's eyes as Moteo continues to slink around him.

None of us dare move.

Ben waves his hand in front of his face to shake off the pungent smell coming from Moteo. He screws his face up, which causes Melanie to chuckle.

Moteo twists round, turning her attention to Melanie.

Melanie's smile fades instantly.

'We know what you're doing!' she challenges Moteo. 'We know about the curse!' Moteo's frame seems to grow bigger. A sickly grin creases her haggard face.

Ben looks horrified when the word *curse* is mentioned.

The trees thrash their branches up and down.

I bite my lip and look across at Melanie. This is not going well.

Moteo points to the children in the valley below. 'Look!' she croaks. 'My children!'

A grin spreads across her face.

'Wow, can anyone kayak?' asks Ben, momentarily distracted by the vast lake behind the BMX track.

Moteo waves her thin arms, inviting him down to the lake below.

Ben bounds down the slope. Melanie hesitates before taking a few measured steps behind him.

'Hey, wait!' I shout to them both. 'Remember why we're here.'

I close my eyes and grit my teeth. Looks like I'm on my own after all.

'Mr Logie knows we're here!' I declare, trying to muster some authority.

Moteo stops, searching for Mr Logie in her memory.

For a second, Moteo's crestfallen features cloud her face.

Then a wheezy, throaty cackle leaves her mouth, and she lurches back and forth.

Peals of thunder echo around the valley, beneath steep cliffs.

I shudder. It's like no other noise!

I look up at the cloudless sky, then towards the rocks where the rumbling seems to come from. It sounds like a giant clearing his throat.

Water tumbles through the rocks, racing in torrents down the hill.

'Robert Logie,' she mutters. 'Gone,' is all she says.

'Why are you doing this?' I demand. 'Taking children, hurting all these people, all these families?'

A picture of Mr Logie's feeble frame tottering about the corridor floods my mind.

Moteo gathers herself and fixes her eyes on me.

The shafts of bright light hold me, as Moteo moves towards me. 'No good!' she snarls.

I scrunch my eyes tight to shut her out. 'He wanted to stop all this!' I shout. 'It's *you* that's not good. You can't take children away from their families!'

Moteo's head bobs about as she quietly chuckles.

'It's not fair,' I say.

'Fair?' She narrows her sparkling eyes.

Down below, two children are pulling at a rope with all their strength. Suddenly one of them collapses, causing the other to fall. Beyond the tug of war, a few girls have skipping ropes. A couple of children roll a hoop with a stick.

It's like going back to a bygone time.

I scurry past her and catch up with Ben and Melanie.

'Wait,' I say, and pull on their arms. 'Don't you see what she's doing? These are the missing children – we've found them!'

Melanie takes a big breath and shakes her head. 'Right,' she snaps, 'let's do it.'

Ben grumbles but joins us. We all head off to where a larger group of people are gathered, watching a football match.

I glance over my shoulder. Moteo is where I left her. Motionless.

As we get closer to the football game, I realise something isn't quite right. No one seems to be moving at any kind of speed. It's all a bit slow. It's nothing like a real football match.

In our games at school, legs and elbows fly, and boots scrape down your shins. There are cuts and bruises, and blood streams down your knee sometimes. But here, no one is even speaking, never mind shouting. No cheering, even when someone scores a goal.

There's no referee either.

And what on earth are they wearing?

TWENTY-EIGHT

The children playing football all have wispy, grey hair. But their faces are the faces of young children, like mine, I suppose.

The football rolls over to where I'm standing. One of the boys shuffles over to fetch it.

I know it's rude to stare, but I can't help it.

He's wearing breeches and stockings that taper to his waist. Never seen anyone dressed like that before!

He stoops to pick up the ball. His skin looks paper-thin. There are wrinkles around his scrawny neck.

'Where are we?' asks Melanie. She gazes around, trying to make sense of what she sees.

Ben is waving his phone about, desperately trying to get a signal. 'Nothing,' he says, dropping his arm.

'Good afternoon,' says the dapper-looking boy, doffing his cap in my direction. He glances across at

Ben, who's still grappling with his phone.

'May I enquire as to what you're holding?' he asks Ben.

'Huh?' grunts Ben.

'I am sorry. Let me introduce myself. My name is Eric,' he says, and bows his head.

Ben clams up, unsure what to make of Eric.

I stare at Eric for a few seconds. He's wearing a sort of neckerchief. His white shirt is slightly grubby. And he's *so* polite.

'They've never seen a mobile before,' says Melanie, shocked.

'What planet have they been living on?' remarks Ben.

'They're all here!' I whisper to Melanie and Ben. '*All* of the missing children. *All* the ones who've disappeared over the years.'

A much older boy – more like a young man – approaches us. 'So, it's a bit like a telephone?' he says, fascinated. 'Simon's the name.'

He smiles and tips his cap. He has knee-length pants with a navy blue striped suit, like a sailor. He's wearing a cloth cap on his head, giving the impression he's about to board a ship.

'Tele…? What's that?' asks Eric.

'A telephone,' explains Simon. He puts his hand to his ear. 'I'm right, aren't I?' He's got a thick beard and his complexion is ruddy. I'm reminded of the sailors on those ships on the school mural.

'What does it do?' asks Eric.

'Here, mine's better,' pipes Melanie, pulling her phone out of her jacket pocket.

'But it still can't get a signal,' says Ben, grinning. 'It's not just a telephone either – you can use it for more than just phoning people.'

'I knew a few posher houses that had telephones,' says Simon. He scratches his head. 'But that thing's so small. How does it work without any wires?'

Melanie and I look at each other. This should be good.

Ben glances briefly at Melanie, who widens her eyes. Ben's on his own with this.

'Well,' Ben begins, 'it's like hundreds of humongous spiders' legs all joined up, passing radio waves to each other.'

Melanie and I stifle a smile.

'It can do loads of things,' Ben continues. 'You can watch programmes on here, the way you do on the telly.'

'Telly? You mean like talking pictures?' asks Simon.

'Mmm, kind of,' Ben replies. 'Only it's a sort of box in the living room now,' he concludes.

'Interesting,' Simon muses. 'I remember people describing talking pictures you could watch in your house. But they were talking about what would happen in the future.'

'So, how long have you been here?' I ask Eric.

'Not long, I think.' He seems puzzled, and looks around the group for help. 'Actually, I'm not sure…'

'You were here before me,' says Simon.

Just then, I spot the large figure of Jonty striding through the crowd. He looks angry.

He stops in front of the gathered group. He folds his arms and eyes me up and down.

'Your phones won't help you in here, squirt,' he says.

There's rage in his eyes. He pushes his twisted face closer to mine. It's like one of those gargoyles on old buildings.

'Nor will Moteo!' he snarls.

Melanie jumps in. 'So, are you captain of this football team?' she asks.

'Course,' snaps Jonty, and puffs out his chest. 'We've got some good players,' he boasts. 'We play football most of the day.' He stares at me. 'And there are no stupid tests to take in here either.'

'Be nice if you could play some away games, though, wouldn't it?' Melanie asks. 'You know, against other teams?'

Jonty turns this over in his mind.

I get what Melanie is trying to do. Really clever! There's a reason why she's top of the league, I guess.

The hunched figure of Moteo stands motionless at the top of the hill. Just in front of the archway. Her cold eyes are fixed on us. A hardened expression is on her face.

'So go on then, get it over with,' I challenge Jonty.

Jonty looks bemused. 'What?' he booms.

'You want to give me a knuckle sandwich. Go ahead,' I simply say.

Jonty moves closer, feet apart.

'Why are *they* here?' Jonty nods towards Ben and Melanie.

'They're my friends,' I say, with a bit of pride.

'Really?' exclaims Jonty. He snorts.

I spot his clenched fist, arms by his side. He looks pumped.

'Pierce and Harrison miss you,' I blurt out. Not sure this is true.

Jonty mulls this over.

'They aren't the same since you've been missing,' I add.

'Humph!' he replies.

I notice Jonty's hands unfurl. He's thinking.

I keep going. 'You shouldn't be here, Jonty,' I say. 'None of these children should be here.'

But as soon as I say it, Jonty's face hardens again. 'You've got some nerve coming back,' he says.

I try and slow down my breathing and say, 'Mr Logie said you've all been trapped.'

'Trapped?' says Jonty incredulously. 'I've only just arrived here!'

'Ten days. That's how long you've been here,' states Melanie.

'No way!' Jonty dismisses the idea. 'I came here with you, Dobbin, right?'

There's no sense of time here. Jonty's lost track of the last ten days.

'You're a time traveller, Jonty. How cool is that?' pipes Ben.

'Time's different in here, I think,' I start to say. But there's not much conviction behind my words.

'*You* can help us,' suggests Melanie.

'Help *you*!' scoffs Jonty. 'To do what?' His jaw is set and I sense the tension in him is beginning to rise again.

A couple more boys stroll over. They were the ones pulling at the rope. One of them has long, uncombed hair. He eyes me with suspicion.

'Who are you?' he snaps.

'Michael,' I reply.

'You know each other then?' He nods to Jonty.

'We're all in the same class,' says Melanie.

The man shrugs. 'Suppose it'll be good to have some new faces in here,' he says.

'What's your name?' asks Melanie.

'Rich,' he says. He puts his hand on the shoulder of the other man. 'Tom and me live on the far side of the valley.'

Tom has a surly expression on his face. His hands are thrust deep inside his pockets. He unnerves me a bit.

Rich senses my apprehension. 'Don't mind him. It gets you down a bit in here, you know?'

'We've come from over there.' Ben looks behind his shoulder at Spinney Wood.

Melanie steps in. 'I think what he means is that we've entered through a portal. Where there's lots of energy allowing people and things to pass through time and space.'

'I was going to say that,' says Ben, convincing no one.

Rich screws up his eyes, straining to see exactly where Ben is referring to.

'Wait…' he says, rubbing his chin. 'Yeah, that's right, I remember now. I lived somewhere else, that's right. I was at school one day, and then…' His words drift away.

'It's a long story,' sighs Melanie.

I see eyes turn away and towards the top of the hill. I watch Moteo as she stumbles down the hill towards us. She can only manage a few steps at a time before she has to stop and rest. So we've still got a bit of time – but not much.

A group of girls have also made their way towards us from the other end of the valley. They stop before they get too close, although one of them steps forward. She smiles shyly at me.

Her thin, wispy hair falls over her shoulders beneath a pretty bonnet. I glance down at her tiny waist. I wonder if she can breathe properly.

'Michael, isn't it?' she asks. 'My name's Doris.'

'Doris?' I splutter. It's an old name. No one's called Doris nowadays.

Her smile widens and then I see cracks appear around her face when she opens her mouth. I look away, a little repulsed.

I realise it may have sounded rude. 'Sorry, I've just never heard of that name,' I say.

Her arms are thin, blue veins pushing through the dry skin. The dress she's wearing goes down to her ankles. But her shoulders are bare, and I see some of her bones protruding.

'It was very popular in my day,' she says, matter-of-fact.

'What, in nineteen hundred?' Jonty laughs sarcastically.

Doris pauses. 'Yes, it was about that time, actually. We were fighting for our rights!' She stamps her foot on the ground.

'Right to do what?' asks Jonty, still smirking.

'To vote, silly.' She rolls her eyes. 'Don't they teach you anything in history nowadays?' she adds.

I glance up at the hill, and Moteo is slowly drawing nearer. We need to move this along quickly.

'Right…' I start, my gaze sweeping over the people in front of me. I try and gather my thoughts. 'Right…' Then I'm stuck for what to say next.

Melanie takes my arm. 'What Michael is *trying* to say is that we need a plan.'

'A plan to do what?' asks Doris, puzzled.

'To get out of here, of course,' says Ben, exasperated.

I take a deep breath. They need to hear the whole truth.

'Moteo was the sole survivor of a massacre years ago. She lost her own family. So, she's been taking children ever since,' I explain.

Ben is about to shout *child catcher* at the top of his voice, when Melanie puts a finger to her mouth.

'She *steals* children,' corrects Ben. He mimics grabbing someone.

'Sort of.' I scrunch my nose at him. 'Thing is, it happens on the anniversary of the battle. Moteo takes a child. It's been happening more and more in recent years.' I glance at Rich and Tom.

'She gets her energy from taking more and more children!' adds Melanie.

'She's like a blood-sucking leech.' Ben wiggles his fingers. It's not helpful.

'I think her world…' I sweep my arm around me, '…all this, gets a burst of energy when new children appear. If we can stop her taking more children,' I plead, 'then all this might just, I don't know, crumble and die.'

'Let me see if I've got this right, young sir?' states Eric. 'We were removed from our families to satisfy Moteo's thirst for *revenge*?' He raises his eyebrows.

'That's pretty much it,' agrees Ben.

I look over my shoulder to gauge Moteo's position and notice the trees have a thicker covering around their trunks. They look stronger; their leaves are greener, brighter even. The grass is fresher, more vibrant; the blades are gently blowing in the breeze. I can hear the cascading water, rushing over the rocks. It's power-building.

'Don't you see? Look at the trees, the water, the grass. The wind has dropped. Even the air smells fresher. It's all because we're here… more children… more energy.'

'We haven't much time,' I go on. 'She'll be here in a few minutes. We have to go *now*.'

'Make it five,' says Tom, keeping a lookout.

'But how?' asks Eric.

'It's like I said. On the anniversary of the massacre, the portal opens.' I hesitate, letting that sink in. 'Remember? You came through a portal?'

But it's too long ago for most of these children. Blank faces stare down at me.

'*Portal*?' repeats Eric.

'Yeah, like a spinning wheel that drags you in, and then spits you out,' explains Ben, rocking from side to side.

'We have a teacher who was here a long time ago. He left when the portal opened,' I explain.

Rich looks puzzled.

'The portal is open for just ten days, because the battle was fought over ten days,' I add.

I need to hurry this up.

'Our teacher, Mr Logie, kept an eye on the portal. He knew the exact date he entered Moteo's world.'

'And when he could leave,' adds Melanie.

'History teacher, smart, eh?' Ben leans forward, tapping his nose.

'Mr Logie chose to tell us everything, knowing he'd fall under the curse,' says Melanie sadly.

'A curse?' asks Simon.

'Moteo's secret must never be shared. It can never be revealed,' I say.

'Why?' asks Simon.

'Once the secret is shared, the curse falls upon you,' I say solemnly.

'On us all,' Melanie adds, gazing around.

'It's her way of keeping her family secret. But it also means no one can stop her. The curse is eating away at him. Mr Logie will...' I hesitate.

'Die!' says Ben starkly.

'Oh, do break the news gently, won't you?' Melanie raises her eyebrows.

Jonty scrunches up his nose.

I shudder at the word, yet know it's true. Mr Logie *will* die.

'He's already really ill, fading away,' I say quietly.

Jonty looks away.

'So what's the plan?' Rich shrugs his shoulders.

This is the tricky bit.

'Thing is, once you're outside, in the real world...' I begin, and then pause.

A sea of perplexed faces turns to me.

'Some of you have been kept alive by all this, this energy... by her!' I say glumly, bowing my head. 'If we destroy her world...' I don't want to finish the sentence.

'Truth is, you're all actually a bit older than you think you are!' Melanie interrupts. She shifts her gaze around the group, to measure their response.

'Just a bit.' Ben rolls his eyes.

There's no easy way to say this.

'Look, I don't know what will happen to you if we get out of here. All of you, well, most of you, are pretty old. Sorry, but the truth is, you may not survive if we leave here.' I bow my head.

Silence.

'If you don't want to come, I understand. I get it. I just thought…' I glance up at the group. 'You might want to help, that's all.'

Doris shuffles forward. 'Well, I'm going to go, for sure. Do what you feel is right, my mother used to say. I'll help Michael!' She smiles.

Eric reaches out, placing his hand on my shoulder. 'Don't worry about us. It's time to put things right. Come on, everyone,' he says.

'What about us?' asks Tom. He furtively glances across at Eric and Simon.

'You've missed out on so much. Having families, jobs,' I say, holding out my hands to the group.

'Getting married.' Eric smiles reflectively.

'Exploring places and climbing mountains,' nods Ben.

'Learning to drive, or going to the cinema,' continues Melanie.

Simon's brow is etched with deep furrows.

'What Michael is trying to say is…' begins Melanie. 'If we make it out of here, you'll never have the chance to do any of those things,' she finishes sadly.

'But you'll be real heroes!' chirps Ben. 'You'll be remembered, by us, at least!'

'We've had a long life, too long, in here,' declares Eric.

'We need to do it for others!' agrees Simon staunchly.

I feel a surge of pride as I seem to be winning them over.

'Look, Moteo! She's nearly here!' says Tom hurriedly. 'And she doesn't look too pleased…!'

'The portal is still open – just!' shouts Melanie.

I check my watch. I blink for a second. It can't be right! It still shows a quarter past four. Not long after we left Mum. Time has stood still since we entered Spinney Wood!

'We'll have a better chance if we split up. She'll be too busy to keep an eye on us all,' I say.

'We can't move too quickly, I'm afraid,' Eric reminds us. 'I get out of breath just walking up and down this football pitch.' He sighs.

'Don't worry,' I say, putting my hand on his shoulder.

'If some of you can leave first, that will weaken her. It will drain her power and give the others the extra time they need to get to the portal,' I add.

'Ben, you need to create a diversion,' I say.

'Huh?' Ben asks. 'How do I do that?'

'Just act normal,' Melanie says with a cheeky smile.

'Once Moteo starts to lose her power, this world will begin to crumble, I think.' I'm not sure this is entirely right, but I'm going with it anyway.

'Sounds like a plan, Master Michael.' Simon clenches his fist.

'That's it? That's your plan?' chirps Tom. 'She won't let us leave. She'll have her own plan.'

'At least we have to try. We have to do something!' I plead.

Tom shoots a glance at Rich. They both nod.

'Is that right about old Logie?' Jonty asks solemnly.

'Afraid so,' I reply.

'But…' He starts to speak.

I can see the wheels turning as he unjumbles his thoughts.

'It didn't really matter if I've gone missing. No one's really missed me,' he says flatly. 'And I wouldn't have to think about all the stuff at home,' Jonty says.

We haven't really got time for this, but I can see Jonty needs to talk.

'What stuff?' I ask.

'It's always been crap at home.' Jonty kicks the football hard. 'My dad died when I was really young,' he continues. 'I've never told anyone because…' He stops talking and for a moment I think he's going to cry. He takes a shallow breath and continues. 'Mum said he was involved in a car accident. He spent weeks in hospital but never recovered. I never got to do things with him. He died when I was seven. That's all I remember of him – that he died.' Jonty's voice fades and he looks straight into my eyes. But there's no malice there.

I reach out and squeeze his arm.

'That must be tough,' I say. 'On your mum as well,' I add.

Jonty mulls this over. He clears his throat and shakes his head.

'I hope he gets better, old Logie, I mean,' he sniffs. He looks relieved. Like a weight has been taken off his shoulders.

'I know I'm a bully. Always picking on little 'uns,' Jonty confesses. 'Don't know why I do it, really.' He shrugs and looks at me for an answer.

I mumble something about *it doesn't matter*. But it does. Jonty wants help with all of this.

'Look, Jonty, we'll try and sort it out when we get out of here. Okay? Maybe talk to the school counsellor?' I say instead.

'Yeah, maybe. Sorry about the stuff with the handkerchief, by the way,' he adds, ducking his chin apologetically.

We smile at each other.

That's a first.

Jonty claps his big hands together noisily.

'C'mon,' he shouts. 'Let's give her a bit of a surprise and taste of her own medicine! What's the plan?'

TWENTY-NINE

We're ready, and not a moment too soon.

Moteo arrives at the foot of the slope, grasping her staff with one hand. The other hand is tucked under her cloak.

'Friends!' she leers, watching us through half-closed eyes.

One by one, children start to break away from the group and follow Ben, who casually starts to head uphill towards the portal.

Moteo studies us all silently, pursing her lips.

Ben whistles as he walks by her, then suddenly veers sideways, wafting away her rank smell.

Simon has a look of contempt on his face as he strolls past Moteo.

Eric keeps his head down, touching his brow as he files past.

Soon, there's a large group of children walking up the hill towards the archway.

Melanie and I, plus a few of the stronger-looking children, stay in the valley, but we fan out, creating a wide space between us.

I wait for the first group to get closer to the portal.

'Stop!' cries Moteo, swinging round to challenge those escaping. She labours up the hill after them.

I wave to Ben. He sees my signal and gets his phone out. Music blasts at full volume from his playlist.

Moteo freezes in bewilderment as Ben starts hopping around like a demented frog to the music. His arms and legs seem to be disconnected from the rest of his body.

'There he goes, sprinkling his fairy dust,' says Melanie, giving a little chuckle.

Moteo struggles to keep Ben in her sight. He's really moving and going wild!

Then we all join in the dance.

Moteo spins round and round, trying to work out what's happening and why everyone is jolting and jerking to the strange sounds. Her eyes flit between the rest of us dancing and Ben's phone. She stumbles over to Ben and tries to grab his phone, but Ben is too quick and dances away, clutching his phone to his chest.

Moteo looks like she's about to explode as she pummels her staff into the ground.

Ben is really winding her up as he thrashes about to the rhythm.

Simon and Eric clap to the beat.

Moteo suddenly takes her hand from under her cloak. She holds something like a glass vial aloft, laughing.

Ben halts.

Eric and Simon stop clapping.

'What's that?' asks Jonty, pointing to the vial.

'It's like an egg timer,' says Melanie. 'My nan used one to time our eggs when I was younger. The sand runs from one end to the other for a set number of minutes.'

Moteo holds the vial higher and we can all see something brown pouring from the top section to the bottom section.

It's earth. Huge chunks of soil fall through the clear glass.

Slowly, a small hole appears in the ground in front of her. The hole widens and a deep chasm appears, separating us into two groups.

I gasp as the gap widens, stretching across the valley.

Peering over the side, my stomach tightens. It's a bottomless pit!

Ben's mouth is wide open as he pulls Simon and Eric away from the edge.

Panic rises in me as the earth is pulled apart, swallowing the hoops, balls and bags that have been discarded in the grass.

'Whoa!' exclaims Jonty.

Everyone takes a step back, away from the massive cavity. There's a stunned silence as we all look at each other in horror.

Moteo chuckles, calmly watching everyone squirm.

She slowly lowers the egg timer, putting her hand back in the tattered cloak.

The grinding sound of the earth halts.

The chasm's too wide to cross. Melanie, Doris, Jonty and I are stuck on this side. Ben, Simon, Eric and the others are on the other side, the one near the portal.

We're trapped.

'Friends!' Moteo hisses in Ben's direction.

Melanie grabs hold of me, clinging to my arm. I quickly disentangle myself, slightly embarrassed.

Moteo's eyes narrow, her gaze boring down on me. She leans heavily upon her staff, rocking back and forth.

Doris steps closer to me.

She pauses. 'You're not going to give up, are you, Michael?' She tilts her head. 'We never gave up when we were marching for our rights. It was very difficult at times,' she reflects, 'but we believed we could change things.' She smiles.

Believe you can change things.

I nod my head and indicate to Ben to carry on towards the portal.

But Moteo has spied them. 'Stop!' Her tiny, thin voice echoes across the chasm, and they stop suddenly in their tracks.

'Fools!' she screams. She slowly lifts her cloak, holding the timer high in the air once more.

My heart skips a beat as I stare at the ground. She isn't finished.

'No!' I shout.

Something that looks like white flakes of snow swirls around in the glass. The snowflakes start to trickle through the timer.

The wind stiffens and the temperature suddenly drops. It's as cold as winter. It's freezing!

I hop on the spot, flinging my arms over my shoulders to keep warm.

I can hardly see across to Ben, Simon and Eric as the snow sleets down in huge draughts.

Doris shivers, hunching her shoulders to try and protect herself.

Moteo lifts her head upwards, basking in her power.

Suddenly she lets out a piercing scream.

Flurries of snow start to fall, large flakes which soon cover the ground. The snow settles and in no time is ankle-deep.

Everyone here's so old and frail. Most of them will be dead in a matter of minutes from hyperthermia.

This is hopeless. I've failed. I've failed Mr Logie. I can't save him. I won't see Uncle Steven or Mum and Dad again.

I've had enough.

'Stop!' I cry.

Moteo twists her head towards me with a look of triumph.

Peering through the driving snow, I watch bodies curling up, sinking onto the ground, their shivering frames covered by even more snow.

I hang my head.

I slump on the floor, hands over my head. The trees thrash their branches, casting off the snow that has settled on them. It lands with a tremendous force on my head. Cold water runs down my neck.

Jonty crouches down next to me and pulls my head out of my hands. 'What do we do now?' he asks in desperation.

THIRTY

I feel a sudden warmth on my skin and turn my head to look at Moteo. She holds the vial aloft, grinning – a sickly grin that turns my stomach.

The snow has melted. Water gushes down in glistening rivulets across the grass.

'Oath binds!' Moteo says, swaying gently and rocking on her staff.

Jonty is still down on his haunches next to me. He starts to flex his muscles.

'You trying to wind her up or summit, mate?' shouts Rich.

'Mine, all mine!' she cackles. 'No one leaves.' She waves the vial at Ben and all the others.

They are so close to the portal.

I need to think clearly. And fast.

The vial is our ticket out of here. But what if it only obeys Moteo?

We could try and destroy it. That might destroy time itself. But what if that destroys us too?

But there is no time here.

Moteo's jaw stiffens as she tightens the grip on her staff. She looks at me suspiciously.

She's got way too much power. We need to get that vial off her.

I notice that Ben's phone has stopped playing music. Its battery must have died.

I've had an idea. 'Quick, Melanie, give me your phone,' I shout to her.

'What for?' she asks. 'I've hardly got any charge left on my phone. It's only good for taking photos.'

'Exactly! Photos! That's it.'

This could work. It has to.

Melanie hands me her phone and I walk close to the chasm's edge.

Ben is rubbing his arm. It looks like he may have hurt it with all that crazy dancing!

'Ben, catch!' I shout, and hurl the phone over to him.

He catches it, just about!

Moteo's eyes follow the phone as it sails through the air.

I hold my forefingers and thumbs together to mimic taking a photo.

Ben stands there, gormless, before he cottons on to what I mean.

He clicks on the camera app, making sure he's not within touching distance of Moteo. He takes her photo.

Ben thrusts the phone in front of her face.

'Look, Moteo,' I shout across. 'You don't want your children to end up like you, do you?'

At first she peers at the screen with confusion. She angles her head different ways, trying to make sense of it. Then her eyes fill with horror and she backs away, afraid.

She glares at Ben and then back to the photo.

'How am I in there?' she cries. 'What have you done to me?'

Moteo snatches the phone out of Ben's hand and drops the vial. She moves it towards her face, trying to understand what's happened.

Ben grabs the vial and moves a few paces away from her.

Moteo is still distracted by looking at her picture on the phone – but for how much longer?

'Here, Ben, to me, to me!' I shout across the chasm. I hold out my hands, ready to catch the vial.

Suddenly Moteo's face twists as she crashes her staff on the ground.

'No good,' she snarls.

I move closer to the edge of the chasm.

Ben hesitates. He rotates his shoulder, rubbing it with his other arm.

Melanie looks at me doubtfully. Ben's not known for his throwing skills… or anything for that matter.

Ben eyes Moteo moving towards him.

I nod to Ben and he tosses the vial.

Melanie and I watch in horror as the vial hovers in the air for a split second.

Then it tumbles into the deep black chasm between us.

THIRTY-ONE

The wind begins to gather force.

A few leaves blow across the ground.

Moteo lets out a deafening wail which echoes around the valley. She clings to her staff as she begins to wobble.

Tiny spots of rain begin to fall.

Darkened clouds hover overhead. Soon, it's tipping down.

The lake swiftly fills with the amount of rainfall spilling.

Without the vial, Moteo's no longer in control of her world.

'We need to go!' Melanie calls out to me.

'I know but how?' I cry, staring out at the huge gap in the earth between us and the route to the portal.

'Go, Ben, leave!' I shout across.

Ben hesitates, unsure what to do.

'Go on! Take everyone and we'll catch up,' I shout, with feigned optimism.

Ben's not convinced, and Eric and Simon stand their ground. 'We can't leave them,' Simon says. 'That would be mutiny.'

'Fools!' Moteo croaks.

Gallons of water gush over the rocks down the hill, crashing onto the ground below. Soon it's crossed the grass and is heading for us, washing into the chasm.

The chasm soon fills with water and becomes a deep river.

We could swim across! But the swirling currents in the water tell me we'd never make it.

The noise of the wind becomes deafening.

A treehouse loses its roof. It whips past me, and I duck to avoid being hit.

Moteo collapses to the ground and gathers her cloak, still clutching Melanie's phone.

There's an almighty *crack* to my left. I turn round and see that a tree has split at its base and fallen forward, close to the chasm.

It's close, but not close enough to make a bridge.

'I've an idea!' I shout above the howl of the wind and the driving rain. 'We'll need your muscle, Jonty,' I say. 'We need to move that tree trunk over the water to make a bridge. Rich, Tom, Doris and Melanie – you'll all have to help.'

Jonty lifts his shoulders, bringing his arms together in a muscle-man pose. The others nod silently.

I cast a look at Moteo. 'She's weakening fast,' I shout. 'This storm is destroying everything. The trees will be the last to go. We need to be ready.'

'Are you sure you know what you're doing, Michael?' Melanie sounds alarmed.

I'm not.

The biting wind whips up tiny sprigs, quickly joined by weak, dead branches that fly through the air. The trees creak as their roots begin to weaken. Their branches snap as the water surges relentlessly around their trunks. The ground starts to shift like sand beneath my feet. I dig my heels in to get a firmer grip.

'Now!' I shout, running over to the fallen tree.

Jonty, Tom, Rich, Doris and Melanie follow.

Water laps around our ankles and is rising. It's starting to spill over from the chasm; soon, this whole valley will be flooded. It will be gone.

'Right, heave as hard as you can. We need to get it over there.' I point to the narrowest point in the chasm.

We shout in pain and frustration as we try and roll the tree forward.

It refuses to budge.

The water is now swirling around our knees and threatens to sweep us off our feet. It's buffeting the trunk and it shifts sideways.

'Together, everything you've got,' I shout. 'One, two, three!'

'Aargh…!' roars Jonty.

Slowly, the tree begins to roll. We keep pushing as it gathers momentum towards the edge of the chasm.

We pause for a breather.

The tree is on its side.

The next bit is the really tricky part. I only hope it's long enough.

We slide the trunk slowly into the water.

We grip the trunk as tightly as we can, as it bobs about.

We wait for a second or two to make sure the trunk won't be suddenly washed away by the swirling water. But no, it holds firm against the edge of the chasm.

For a second, I'm afraid the tree won't reach the other side of the bank. But it fits beautifully.

As if it was made for it.

Jonty gently squeezes my arm.

Ben, Eric, Simon and the others turn and make their way down the hill.

It's difficult manoeuvring across the trunk. Although it's wide enough, the wind keeps buffeting me, making it tricky to balance.

'Don't try to walk – just sit down and shuffle your bottom across,' I yell back at the others, who are following me.

Ben, Eric and Simon hold the trunk as steady as they can.

'Okay, I think we've got it,' Ben shouts across the fast-flowing river.

I make it to the other side first – Rich is next, then

Tom and Melanie. I wait for Doris and the others. Then there's Jonty at the rear.

Doris is really struggling. She collapses on the trunk, her tired body beaten by the effort.

'Don't look down,' I warn her. 'I'm coming to help you.'

I hold out my hand to Doris and take her weight as she inches her way across the trunk.

'Just keep going,' Jonty shouts. 'Not far now.'

The water is rising fast. It laps around the edge of our makeshift bridge.

Jonty is the last to cross the chasm. We all wrap our arms tightly around the trunk at the other end to make sure it's secure. Jonty carefully makes his way across.

The trunk at Jonty's end is beginning to move back and forth. The sudden movement is causing Jonty to lose his balance.

As Jonty nears us, the end of the trunk is wrenched out of our hands by the force of the water.

'Jonty!' I scream. I reach out my hands and grab hold of his arm.

We all haul him up the bank as the water suddenly hurls the trunk down the raging river.

We hug each other briefly and then catch up with the others making their way up the hill.

I look back down the valley and see Moteo sprawled across the muddy ground, her world crumbling about her.

The sky is now pitch-black. Booming thunder shakes the valley.

The torrent of water in the chasm has now broken its banks. With a roar, the water sweeps over Moteo and she's lost from sight.

She's still clutching Melanie's phone.

I spy her staff floating to the surface.

'Let's go,' I say to Jonty.

THIRTY-TWO

Storm clouds crash around my ears as I push my soaked body through the portal.

Suddenly there's only an eerie silence.

Stillness.

The sun is flitting through the trees. Birdsong announces the dawn.

I check my watch. I can't believe it's morning!

A cold mist covers the wood.

The archway has disappeared. It's gone.

Eric and Simon stand wide-eyed as they look around them.

'So, I guess this is it?' Simon says.

'Spinney Wood?' asks Doris incredulously.

'Spinney Wood,' I nod.

'I used to come here with my mother,' Doris reminisces.

Melanie bites her lip.

'You've done it,' says Eric. 'You've broken the chain.'

'No, *we* have.' I smile. 'Team effort, eh?'

We shake hands. Eric's bony fingers have little strength.

'I would have quite liked to get to know you, young sir,' Eric says. He blinks away a tear.

Rich slaps my shoulders. 'Thanks, mate,' he says. Even Tom has a faint smile on his lips.

Suddenly Tom and Rich gasp in pain.

They grow taller before my eyes. Their shoulders broaden and they both sprout bushy beards.

I can't believe the transformation!

They've become men.

Ben is open-mouthed. He runs both hands over his own body, checking for a similar growth spurt.

Melanie rolls her eyes at him.

The rest of the group are tottering around, barely managing to stand.

They're cold and shivering.

'Thanks, Captain,' Simon salutes me. 'You're made of stern stuff, make no mistake,' he says admiringly.

It seems as though I've known them longer than one night.

Time's a funny thing.

Doris turns shyly to Jonty. 'Make sure you learn your history,' she teases him.

Jonty gulps hard, nodding.

Melanie rubs a hand across her tearful eyes.

The cold, still air is biting. I can see Doris and the others are struggling to breathe. They huddle together for warmth. Mist envelops them and begins to erase their fragile bodies.

'No!' cries Melanie, starting to stop them.

I hold her arm, shaking my head.

Slowly, Eric's and Simon's faces recede into the mist, slowly disappearing with a smile.

Doris waves energetically, her thin, white hair absorbed by the clinging mist.

I glance at Melanie, her cheeks wet with tears.

I grab her and Ben and the three of us hug each other, right there in the middle of Spinney Wood.

'We did it,' I say with a cheer.

We break apart and I spot Jonty, standing to one side, looking awkward.

I gesture to him, and we share another group hug, this time welcoming Jonty into our embrace. A big grin lights up his face.

Another first for me and Jonty, I guess.

There's a wail of sirens and we spot uniformed officers striding towards us through the woods. Some are leading dogs that are straining at the leash.

'So what's the story then?' asks Rich. 'What do we tell them? They'll want to know what's happened. Who we are? Where we've come from?'

'We could just say nothing… for now anyway,' I suggest.

'They'll work out who you are from old photos,' says Melanie. 'Plenty of time for that once we get out of these woods.' She looks around and shudders.

A snap of broken twigs interrupts our conversation.

A plainclothes police officer is looking straight at Jonty. 'Glad you're safe, lad,' he smiles. 'You been in these woods all this time?'

'Yeah, I'm pretty good at hiding. Sorry I've caused you all that trouble. I just needed a bit of space,' Jonty says.

'Well, you can explain that to your mother, eh?' the police officer says, before turning to Rich and Tom.

'Do I know you two?' He angles his head, taking a long hard look at both men.

'Yeah, probably. We've been working around town. Casual like, mostly. Cash in hand,' Rich replies.

The police officer nods his head slowly, but I see he's not convinced.

Melanie, Ben and I keep quiet.

Warm blankets are thrown round our shoulders. A doctor quickly gives us the once-over.

Police tape is hastily rolled out around the scene, sealing it off from the public. Two police officers guard the area.

But there's nothing to be seen. No sign of an archway. The trees are resolutely silent.

I hear a familiar voice. Two figures are running towards us.

Mum is waving frantically as she spots me.

She makes a funny sort of primal scream and flings her arms round me. Dad holds us both as we stand together in the middle of the wood.

THIRTY-THREE

We're driving over to see Uncle Steven.

He's in a residential home now. I thought those places were only for old people, but Mum says they're also for people who can't cope at home.

It's only on the other side of town so we can see him as much as we want.

It's like one huge bungalow. A smiley nurse greets us. She says she'll bring Mum and Dad a cup of tea in a bit. We can pop into her office and ask her anything after the visit.

A cheerful bright carpet lines the corridor. We pass one resident walking with a frame, helped along by a carer. They both look happy and say hello.

We arrive at Uncle Steven's room. Pushing the door open, Mum tentatively enters in case he's asleep.

'Oh, hello, you lot. I wondered if you'd be coming today,' he says.

His face is leaner, and I can see he's left some of his breakfast uneaten.

Mum kisses him on his cheek. Dad shakes his hand.

The television is on. It's in the corner, but it's on mute. You can see the garden from his window.

Mum's brought some flowers.

'How are you settling in?' Mum asks.

'Well, it could do with a few piccies to brighten it up,' he says, looking round the room. 'I can't complain. The staff can't do enough for me. But that's enough about me… what's this I hear about you, Michael? Or should I say Inspector Dobson from the Yard?' He picks up a newspaper from his lap and waves it in front of me. The headline reads *Missing Children Found by Schoolboy*.

'Well, who'd have thought it?' He beams at me. 'My little nephew, a national hero.'

'It was the three of us actually,' I admit.

'Ah, but you were the main man,' he says, and digs an elbow towards me. 'You must be so proud of him,' Uncle Steven says to Mum and Dad.

'Of course we are!' Mum replies. She ruffles my hair. 'But even heroes need a haircut.' She laughs.

'He'll probably get loads of offers now from his adoring public,' smiles Dad.

'What?' says Mum.

'Girls, of course! If I know anything, they'll be lining up outside the door,' Dad says.

'What would you know about loads of offers?' Mum teases him.

'Nothing, my dear. There was only ever you!' Dad replies, and winks at her.

They're both in playful mode. They've been getting on so much better recently. The counselling sessions seem to be helping. I've even been to one of their appointments with them. I know their disagreements have nothing to do with me.

Mum squeezes my hand.

She sits down on the edge of Uncle Steven's bed and starts to cry softly.

It takes us all by surprise.

'You know, Steven, I'm so sorry about your accident,' she says. 'If only I hadn't…' She doesn't get the chance to finish the sentence before Uncle Steven places his finger to her lips.

'Debs, don't. It was never your fault. It was just an accident, that's all. There's nothing to forgive. Except… you need to forgive yourself, eh?' He leans over and plants a gentle kiss on her cheek. He squeezes her arm.

Mum sighs and gives a watery smile.

'I know,' she says. 'Time to move on… for all of us.' She takes a deep breath.

I momentarily think of Mole and Jack Flash. Time they moved on too, I reckon. In fact, I think they've already left.

Uncle Steven winks at me as he closes his eyes.

We stay for a little while in case Uncle Steven wakes.

But he's soon snoring.

THIRTY-FOUR

'So, what do you think, blue or black?' asks Mum. She's holding two pairs of shoes.

She's wearing a dress she hasn't worn for yonks.

'Er, blue,' says Dad. He's posing in front of the mirror, trying to comb his thinning locks.

'You're not even looking!' Mum frowns. 'What do you think, Michael?' She sighs.

I'm glad I only have one pair of shoes.

She doesn't wait for my answer and rushes out to the hallway.

'Michael, hurry up and get changed,' she calls. 'We can't be late.'

I'm glad Melanie and Ben will be there at the Town Hall for the ceremony. At least I won't have to say anything. This hero thing is embarrassing.

Still, it is nice to be recognised for rescuing Jonty.

As we drive through the nearby streets, I start to get nervous.

My hair won't sit down so I don't even try. I feel uncomfortable in my formal jacket and trousers.

We arrive at the Town Hall and are greeted by a uniformed police officer.

'Welcome, Mr and Mrs Dobson,' he says with a big smile. 'Michael!' he exclaims, staring at me intently. 'Well, we meet at last! I've only read about you and seen your photograph up until now.'

He escorts us past reception into a large carpeted hall. It's very posh. Lots of people are already sitting down. A few of them turn round and smile at me.

I look up at the big stage and spy two familiar faces.

I wave to Melanie and Ben. They half wave back. An official-looking woman is showing them where to stand and what to do during the presentation part of the ceremony.

I join Melanie and Ben on stage and take a note of where we've got to sit, stand and walk during the ceremony. It feels strange sitting on the front row of the stage, but it gives us a great view of everyone arriving.

Mum and Dad are in one corner talking to someone important in a suit.

'This is so cool,' enthuses Ben. 'Maybe there'll be some TV producers here, who'll want to sign us up for a film deal.'

'Oh, yeah, that's very logical, here in Longfields. Hollywood, here we come,' says Melanie, and rolls her eyes.

'Use your imagination. Anything could happen,' he says, with a gleam in his eye.

Melanie and I smile at each other.

'You're right, Ben,' I agree. 'Anything can happen.'

'Especially when you're on manoeuvres,' Melanie adds, and we all laugh.

I watch the clock slowly wind its way to two o'clock.

Suddenly I see a man wearing an orange scarf striding into the hall.

It's Mr Logie!

He waves to me from the back of the hall. He looks happy. He looks well. And he's walking fine!

Mum and Dad are sitting in the front row, both beaming. Mum has got her phone ready to take photos.

The chattering in the hall stops as the Chief Inspector gets to his feet. He moves closer to the lectern.

'It gives me great pleasure to meet three very special people today. Three people who risked their own safety to rescue a friend.'

I'm slightly taken aback at the thought of Jonty as a friend.

Maybe he is now.

There's a sudden flurry of clicks and flashes as a few photographers start taking pictures.

I shift uneasily in my seat and lower my head, so I don't have to look at anyone.

The photographers sit down again and the Chief Inspector continues.

'All three pupils are from Longfields School, which

can be rightly proud of producing such fine young men and women. Ladies and gentlemen, may I give you Ben Gillet, Melanie Smithson and Michael Dobson.' The Chief Inspector puts his hands together and the hall echoes with generous applause.

We file up to the lectern and receive our certificates of commendation from the Chief Inspector. He shakes our hands firmly before standing back to let the photographers take more pictures of us.

I can't help clicking my heels together. Need to stop them in case anyone hears.

I steal a glance at Mum. She is holding Dad's hand.

Ben is reading his certificate and has already got it framed and hanging in his room.

'Let's give these young people another round of applause,' the Chief Inspector says.

Melanie leans across and whispers, 'I guess we're all top of the league today.'

'You bet,' I say.

The clapping starts up again and I can feel my heart pumping zillions of pints of blood.

I look up at Mum and Dad, who are on their feet.

I hear a loud *whoop, whoop* from somewhere in the audience. It's coming from a man in a wheelchair who's in the middle of the aisle. I can't believe it! Uncle Steven is here! He's supported by his carer, who's also clapping. She wheels him up to sit next to Mum and Dad.

Dad gives me the thumbs-up. Mum gets out a

handkerchief to dab at her tears. She rubs Uncle Steven's arm and he pats it with his hand.

Melanie, Ben and I sit down again and the Chief Inspector gives a short talk about personal safety. I can see Mum nodding solemnly to his speech.

It's turning out to be the best day ever!

Ben is still posing for a few more pictures as people are leaving the hall. He's in his element. I wouldn't be surprised if he was passing on survival techniques to them.

Uncle Steven is waiting patiently to hug me. It looks like it's made his day as well, to be here.

Mum and Dad walk over to chat with Melanie's and Ben's parents. I'm slightly worried Mum will say something embarrassing about me. Best not to think about it. At least she's not carrying her notebook.

Uncle Steven taps me on my arm. 'Has the Chief Inspector signed you up for his team? After cracking this case, you're bound to be in demand. If you need an agent, I might know someone.' He winks.

'I'm so glad you're here,' I say, hugging him again.

'I wouldn't miss it for the world, maestro!' he says with a chuckle.

Melanie gives me a wave and a thumbs-up as she leaves the hall. 'See you in history,' she mouths.

'See you,' I mouth back, and grin.

'Nice girl, that Melanie,' Dad says. 'She was telling me she plays football. So guess what! We've arranged a game on Saturday in the park. Ben's coming too.'

Unbelievable!

Melony Magic, Great Goliath and Wizard's Troops are on the move!

Should be some game!